Airship 27 Productions

The Challenger Chronicles Volume One

"The Secret History of Renswick Vale" © 2023 Gordon Dymowksi
"The Desert of the Lost" © 2023 Barbara Doran
"What Rough Beast" © 2023 Michael Panush
"The Unseen Star' © 2023 Samantha Lienhard

Published by Airship 27 Productions
www.airship27.com
www.airship27hangar.com

Interior and cover illustrations © 2023 Clayton Hinkle
Back cover illustration by Harry Roundtree from "The Lost World" by Arthur Conan
Doyle.

Editor: Ron Fortier
Associate Editor: Fred Adams Jr.
Marketing and Promotions Manager: Michael Vance
Production Designer: Rob Davis

ISBN: 978-1-953589-56-9

Printed in the United States of America

10 9 8 7 6 5 4 3 2 1

the Challenger
Chronicles
Volume One

TABLE OF CONTENTS

The Secret History of Renswick Vale
By Gordon Dymowski

In the two years since our journey to South America, my relationship with Professor George Challenger had taken a more cordial yet professional tone. I had been assigned by the Daily Gazette to chronicle Challenger's efforts with great success, and my relative good fortune has provided greater freedom and renown. As a result, the name "Ned Malone" has greater cache and my documentation of the work of Professor George Edward Challenger serves as a testament of one man's efforts to bring logic and reason into an ever-chaotic world.

Since our trip to South America, Challenger had taken up a new career as a "consulting scientist", working with His Majesty's Government, Parliament, and other related offices providing advice and consultation. One such institution was the Royal Astronomical Society, who had provided a small stipend for Professor Challenger to study Halley's Comet using new equipment from a physicist in France. Seeing an opportunity for both personal and professional refreshment, I eagerly packed my things and accompanied Challenger to the small, unobtrusive English village of Renswick Vale.

So it was on this rather late morning on a Tuesday that I found myself dumbstruck in observing Challenger having an open argument with a rival. We were sitting in the dining-room of a small inn outside of the village. It was a small room with a table capable of holding a small number of guests, and our funders had essentially rented out the entire place for a four-day period. Our morning began with an informal breakfast consisting of buttered eggs, toast, assorted pastries, fruit, and copious amounts of coffee. Except for one seat, the room was bursting to capacity. Challenger himself was a large, boisterous man with an Assyrian-trimmed beard, dark hair, and equally piercing eyes.

As his outsized frame struggled within the narrow confines of his chair, Challenger leaned forward and pointed his toast in an accusing manner at our current dining companion. As Challenger spoke, the thin man with dark, thinning hair ignored the half-eaten plate in front of him.

Oblivious to the crumbs in his own beard, Challenger pointed his toast as he spoke with rancor, "Confound it, Drake! I don't care about your tenure—this is a once-in-a-lifetime chance to gain valuable scientific insight!"

Sitting back in his chair, Jonathon Drake regarded Challenger with the stillness of a surgeon. Dressed in the modest accouterments of his fellow Oxford historians, Drake's frame never shifted in his chair. Perhaps it was one of the reasons for his reputation as a difficult teacher and even more difficult individual. Despite Challenger's obvious agitation, Drake's steely eyes never wavered, and the mood conveyed by his angular features seemed almost accusatory.

In a clipped, cold authoritative voice Drake answered, "Listen, Challenger, I don't know what kind of doggerel they taught you at...*Edinburgh*...but my colleagues and I believe in the immutable fact of history! I prefer to focus on the actual activities of people and the forces that drive them. You look to the stars for salvation...I look to *humanity*."

Placing his toast on his empty plate, Challenger bellowed, "That is why Malone and I are *here!* Look at what's happening in the Balkans—the 'powder keg of Europe', as the papers say—and we want to believe in something bigger, something nobler. All you want to do is keep your attention to dusty records and believe you're trying to find something noble. Malone and I have seen the truth in South America—history is *alive*. We are making it! And studying the comet will lead us towards the future!"

"Just because some amateur astronomer named Halley discovered a comet does not make it important..." A sharp grin rose on Drake's face. "...except as a way of marking seventy-some years. The future is always taking shape, but the past is immutable. Documented. Unlike you, Challenger, I place my faith in facts and records. That way, I do not have to worry about *my* efforts being published in one of London's tawdriest rags by a glorified schoolboy!"

Sudden courage rose within me as I found myself asserting, "I will have you know, good sir, that I work hard to represent *all* of Professor Challenger's activities with great accuracy! The fact that Mr. Challenger has not stooped so low as to offer personal insults speaks more to his strength of character than your apparent lack of one!"

A brief glimpse of a smile played upon Challenger's face as he turned to me. After a brief glance, he turned back and pointed his finger at Drake, "Suffice it to say, Mr. Drake, that Mr. Malone has endeavored to chronicle my experiences in an even-handed manner. After all, *you* were the one who was spouting about the 'immutability of history', remember?"

Raising his palms in a defensive manner, Drake spoke in a patronizing tone, "There, there, Challenger...It is bad enough you and I have to share a room, board, and resources. My only purpose here is to research a village with little—if any—recorded history. My specialty is the early Tudor period, most notably Henry VIII, and Renswick Vale was founded by a group of Catholics after England broke with the Catholic Church. It remained unscathed when the Witchcraft Act of 1537 was enabled—"

"Bah, witchcraft!" Challenger blurted. "I am sure that Mr. Malone knows more—"

"And that is my point precisely!" Becoming more animated, Drake seemed to gloat at Challenger's statement. "This is a hidden village with minimal contact with London *or* the outside world. Except for some early correspondence in the first five years of the village—"

"There is no recorded history whatsoever..." I asserted. "At least, not in London. Researchers at the Royal Astronomical Society worked with several historians. Although this is the perfect site to observe and record Halley's Comet with clear skies and no geographic interference, there are no documents outside of that first five years of the village's existence."

"That is why I am *here*, my good man," Despite his efforts, Drake sounded counterfeit in his assertion of good will, "Very few people have visited Renswick Vale, much less decided to reside here. Those who make this village their home never leave. In my initial conversations with the townspeople, there is no one 'in living memory' who can recall the town's entire history. They have suggested that I speak with a man named Hulke—Roderick Hulke—who serves as the town's librarian and record keeper.

"No records?" Challenger nodded as I asked Drake, "Is that not...unusual?"

"Given the early history of the village, Mr. Malone," Despite the obvious schoolmaster's tone in his voice, Drake displayed genuine curiosity. "It is understandable. After all, people came here to avoid persecution—why bring attention to themselves? But one of the unique qualities of Renswick Vale has been its isolation and the fact that its first settlers perceived...how did that letter describe it...?"

Challenger blurted before I could answer, "A 'shower of light' leading to a 'beacon of hope.' John Renswick, town founder, 1536 letter to his sister. Except for some witch trials in the 1600s, nothing of note. You've spent enough time bragging of your discoveries, Mr. Drake."

"The large marble tower standing in the middle of the town square serves as the 'beacon of hope'." As Drake's chest expanded, tones of pride and arrogance crept back into his voice. "Carved from an outcropping of rock...but after my previous project involving reconstructing the history of a 'lost' Chinese village with my assistant, Miss Chen, I thought it might be advantageous to study and formally document the history of Renswick Vale. Imagine how surprised *I* was to find that I was competing for work space with Challenger and his off-handed stargazing project!"

As irritation lined his face, Challenger moderated his tone; "This is a once-in-a-lifetime chance for the Royal Astronomy Society to gather data on Halley's Comet. Although there are astronomers tracking its position, *my* purpose is to determine the exact emanations from a celestial body. This village has a clear view and perception, allowing us to use very specialized equipment."

"Scientific claptrap!" Drake's tone was clipped and abrupt. "There is barely enough room for the both of us to work, much less including your 'instruments'. *I* am pursuing a course that will build my academic reputation; *you* are nothing more than a charlatan and a huckster!"

Although I attempted to reason with Drake, Challenger cut me off, "It is fortunate, good sir, that we all have separate rooms. Given your behavior, I will brook *no* insult from you or Miss Chen—"

"Please," A female voice emerged from behind me. "Call me Diana."

Both Professor Challenger and I rose from our chairs and turned to greet our new guest. She was tall and modestly dressed in a white blouse and a long, black skirt. Everything about her aspect appeared well-composed: her black hair was tied into a bun, and the wire-framed spectacles did nothing to interfere with her oval face and a slightly tan complexion. Only Drake remained seated, wearing a look of contempt and disgust at his assistant on his face.

After making introductions to Challenger and me, Diana sat and selected her breakfast items. Her plate consisted of buttered eggs, fruit, and toast. As she began eating, she flashed a smile at both Challenger and myself. As we smiled back, Drake shot her a glance which resulted in a slight stiffening of her posture, but nothing more.

Something about Challenger softened as he regarded Diana. Perhaps he was reminded of his own wife and daughter, or perhaps he was reminded that Sir John Roxton was currently traveling towards China and Japan at His Majesty's request. It was not my place to speculate, so I did not inquire.

In a tone suggesting petulance, Drake offered, "Before you chose to *insult* me, Challenger, I should point out *why* my project is important. Except for a few letters from John Renswick, the town's founder...there is little, if any, history of the first one hundred and forty years of this village!"

Rising from his chair, Challenger had a demonic glint about him as he snarled, "I don't *care* about the trivialities of life here, nor do I believe such matters warrant serious study. However, the comet can tell us all about the nature of the cosmos, of our existence...we can see a glimpse of the totality of the universe in a microcosm!"

Glancing around the table, I found that the innkeeper and her assistants were avoiding us. As I turned towards Diana, she gave me a look that spoke layers of understanding. We were both familiar with dealing with difficult men.

Speaking in a calm, cool voice, Diana managed to calm Challenger down, "You may be missing the point, Professor Challenger...your comet and this village share one thing: a *history*. Experiences, moments, even phenomena that are left unexamined. There is a great mystery waiting to be uncovered."

Lowering his bulky frame into his chair, Challenger flashed a warm grin at Diana. Turning towards me, he nodded his approval of the woman.

"Perhaps you can tell us more?" I asked, following Challenger's lead and wishing that I had remembered to bring my notebook. Obviously displeased, Drake simply took a small sip of coffee and beheld all three of us in silent contempt.

Adjusting her posture, Diana spoke in a well-learned, assertive tone, "It is one of the lessons I learned working with Mr. Drake...that every place, every moment, has a history.....a *secret* history. That history is a collection of tales never told, thoughts never expressed, and matters never spoken out loud but only in whispers, hidden by the shadows of larger forces. That history can be found in details...in both the minutiae of documents and through the stories and tales told by those who live in the aftermath of that history."

Despite Drake's visible disapproval, Diana sipped her coffee and continued, "Your comet, Professor Challenger, only comes once in a lifetime. This town has a rich history...much of which is missing. Both you and Mr. Drake share a similar goal: uncover untold stories. There is much about that goal that is noble, inspiring, and *heroic*."

As outrage soured the look on his face, Drake clapped slowly, "Bravo, Miss Chen! I'm sure that Challenger will give you good marks for not rehashing that 'shower of light' and 'beacon of hope' claptrap. After all, many of *your* kind believe in that superstitious mumbo-jumbo..."

With a sudden jolt from his chair, Challenger faced down Drake and declared in a hushed, sinister tone, "Listen to me, my *good* sir...that kind of ignorant drivel is unwelcome in my presence!"

Rising with one sharp movement, Drake faced Challenger and confronted him, "You *listen*...much like your lackey Mr. Malone, Miss Chen is *privileged* to work with me. They are both here at *our* convenience, neither one having earned their reputation or their position."

If there is one thing Challenger would never brook, it was slander of his reputation. Insulting me was, by extension, insulting him. Despite his arrogance and foul temper, Challenger had a heroic heart.

"Let me advise you, Mr. Drake....tread *wisely,*" Glancing at Diana and me, Challenger addressed Drake with concern. "Between Mr. Malone's colleagues at the *Gazette* and my colleagues at Oxford, there is enough to warrant a public inquiry into your activities. As far as I am concerned, Miss Chen is a valued colleague, and I am hopeful that we *all* can work together."

Seeing Challenger flash her a grin as he returned to his seat, Diana addressed Drake, "And besides...there is a column in the middle of the town square named the Beacon of Hope. I have earned my reputation—and my position—without your assistance, and I will not brook your patronizing manner nor will I endure your arrogant posturing!"

Exchanging glances, Challenger and I agreed on Diana's behavior. Given that we rarely agreed on matters, this was extremely significant.

Although irritation briefly flashed on his face, Drake took on a tone of counterfeit attrition, "Do not be so impertinent, young lady..."

Just then, a man entered the room; he was tall with angular features and a head of sparse brown hair with several streaks of gray. He was wearing the familiar blue and gold button uniform of a policeman.

"Which one of you is Professor George Edward Challenger?" he asked.

Rising from his chair, Challenger approached the officer and extended his hand. Rather than return the handshake, the officer asked, "Do you have any medical training?"

"Yes...I studied medicine in Edinburgh," Stumbling somewhat, Challenger seemed off-put by the question.

Shaking Challenger's hand, the police officer said, "My name's Burgess. We need you at the station."

Glancing back towards us, Challenger noted my and Diana's interest as well as Drake's apathy.

Turning back towards Burgess, Challenger asked, "What do you need me for?"

Burgess rubbed the back of his neck, "Strange circumstances."

Turning back towards us, Challenger stated, "Miss Chen, Mr. Malone... please accompany me. I believe you both might be of assistance."

I recognized Challenger's statement as an attempt to provide some respite for Diana. Nothing in her demeanor suggested reluctance as she rose from her chair. As I joined Challenger and Diana as we followed Burgess from the dining room, we left Drake to finish his breakfast in solitude.

There was nothing pleasant about the makeshift laboratory in the corner room of the constabulary. Like many villages of its type, Renswick Vale had no formal coroner. Although their usual procedure included having the funeral director examine the corpse, the grisly and unusual nature of this crime made it more appropriate for Challenger's more clinical and scientific disposition. As Diana and I watched from afar, we stood in the white-walled room for an hour as Challenger examined a body on a table.

Various apothecary and chemical equipment lined the shelves of the makeshift laboratory. Several instruments on a table close to Challenger were obviously makeshift approximations of the tools that Challenger had used in the past. Both Diana and I had glimpsed, but not examined the corpse; nothing about it stood out except for the large stains of blood on the front of the shirt and the lumped, misshaped facial features. Two men were quietly conferring with Challenger: one of them was Burgess, and the other was a tall yet portly man with gray hair. Despite his girth, his blue button-down uniform had a perfect fit on his frame, and the gold star pinned to his chest possibly indicated authority.

As Burgess left, Challenger and the portly officer approached the two of us. As Challenger removed the gloves from his hands, the officer regarded us with curiosity, especially Diana.

"Constable Reginald Hinchcliffe," Introducing himself, the man extended his hand. "Glad to meet you."

As he shook my and Diana's hand, nothing about him suggested authority. After placing the gloves on a nearby shelf, Challenger approached us and declared, "I'm sorry, Constable, but this is nothing more than a man beaten to death. In fact, the only notable thing is that this appeared to be a savage, violent attack."

"Well, here's the thing that I find notable," Hinchcliffe's tone suggested outrage as he pointed to the corpse on the table. "Roderick Hulke. Our town librarian and record keeper. Never married, never a problem. Kept to himself, mostly. There's *no* reason why *anyone* would attack him like that."

"Town librarian *and* record keeper?" I asked.

"What kind of records?" Diana followed up.

Hinchcliffe flinched, "Yes, he *was* the town record keeper...we don't have much of a rationale why; just that at some point, it was determined that the librarian would also keep track of other matters. Maybe it was in response to persecution, maybe the result of the witch trials..."

Arching an eyebrow, Challenger asked, "Witch trials? *Here?*"

Shifting his posture, Hinchcliffe sighed, "We were founded by Catholics trying to keep silent and away from royal sight. Our leaders made a decision."

Taking a step out of Hinchcliffe's sight, Challenger mouthed *he doesn't know.* Catching his meaning, I kept silent.

"But that's not the strangest thing..." Hinchcliffe remarked. "The strangest is that Nicholas Burton, the man who beat him—is the quietest, calmest man you might ever know. The only problem that barrister had with Hulke concerned an overdue book. And the funny part...Burton turned *himself* in, claiming that he didn't remember what happened...only that he awoke next to Hulke's corpse."

"Where were both men?" Diana asked.

"Next to the Beacon," Hinchcliffe said, surprised by Diana's seeming impertinence.

"Perhaps I should talk to him..." Challenger mused aloud.

"Won't do you any good," Hinchcliffe said with a tone of authority. "He remembers *nothing.*"

As his chest rose and fell in a *harrumph*, Challenger stated plainly, "I will be the judge of that. What you may not understand, Constable is that my expertise in the scientific might provide a rationale for Burton's sudden explosion of temper."

After scratching his chin in the way that one does when avoiding a direct answer, Hinchcliffe shrugged, "All right...come this way, Challenger...but only you."

Before stepping away, Challenger whispered to us, "Mr. Malone, would you please accompany Miss Chen to—never mind...?"

As Challenger turned and walked towards Hinchcliffe, I realized that he was reacting to the look of disapproval on Diana's face. At that moment, her reaction was understandable, but I refused to dwell on matters. Seeing Challenger and Hinchcliffe walk through the door towards the holding cell, Diana and I left the constabulary onto the streets of Renswick Vale.

Renswick Vale was a placid, quaint village that at first glance appeared rather innocuous and bland. Nothing about the village seemed distinctive, with various structures and buildings seemingly placed at random. People made their way through the streets of the village in silence, with only a few moments of interaction. As we made our way through, some villagers regarded Diana with a mixture of curiosity and suspicion. After all, many of them had probably never known a Chinese person outside of Fleet Street's torrid articles and tawdry, poorly written half-penny periodicals. My travels with Challenger had broadened my perspective enough to accept others; that attitude had not made its way outside of London despite our renown.

Making our way to the center of town, Diana pointed out a large tower in the center of the square. All of the houses and structures of the village surrounded the alabaster tower. Shaped like a chess piece, the square base had the words BEACON OF HOPE carved on one side. Standing eleven feet tall, the Beacon was cylindrical in shape, smooth to the touch and lightly veined with gray. At the top of the beacon was a multifaceted carving that came to a point; it resembled a poor attempt to carve something that appeared like a flame. Oblivious to the large tower, the people of Renswick Vale went about their day.

Keeping silent, both Diana and I examined the Beacon lost in thought. Neither one of us wanted to address the horrible sight of Hulke's battered corpse in the midst of such a placid town. Within moments, we glanced at each other sharing silent sadness.

Turning back towards the Beacon, Diana related, "This is it. Carved from an outcropping of rock discovered by the Catholic settlers in 1536. Guided by a—"

"*Shower of light,*" Remembering previous comments, I decided to engage Diana. "Does anyone know where this rock—"

Diana's voice had an irritated tone, "Mr. Drake spoke with several geologists who had no idea where this rock came from. This stone has been here since Roman times, and their records noted that the tribal Brigantes avoided this area."

"Why?"

"Those manuscripts are...incomplete," Diana's shoulders tensed slightly. "They suggest that the Brigantes were simply...afraid of the rock. This area had been desolate woodland until the town was settled by John Renswick and his followers."

An elderly woman shuffled by, delivering a poisonous glance at Diana. Diana's lack of response betrayed the look of discomfort on her face.

In an effort to learn more about my new colleague and develop a professional relationship, I asked, "Pardon my curiosity, but I thought I heard that you helped Drake on—"

"Translating some manuscripts from the 'lost' village in Shanxi," Relieved at my casual tone, Diana opened up. "My grandparents were originally from

"Does anyone know where this rock—"

that province and had taught me the dialect. When Drake discovered that 'lost' village, he reached out to my parents' apothecary in Limehouse..."

Noticing my interest, Diana further related, "They sent me to some really great schools—they could pay, after all—and Drake recruited me after I left secondary school. My payment is an Oxford education at no cost...except for my time."

"It must be challenging," I stated.

"Not as much as dealing with Challenger," Smiling at her unintended pun, Diana gradually warmed to me as she spoke. "I know his reputation. I *have* read the papers."

We smiled at each other, basking in the glow of a blossoming friendship. However, Challenger's harsh tone broke our reverie.

"Confounded jackanapes!" Bristling with outrage, Challenger released his full fury onto the both of us. "That man came close to ruining our experiments!"

"What happened?" I was reluctant to hear the answer.

Regaining his composure, Challenger remarked, "First, that infernal Drake came close to discarding the special wrappings that covered our equipment."

Noting Diana's confusion, I noted, "These are lined with lead, I believe, in order to prevent stray radio-activity from affecting their readings."

"Not only *that*," Tightening his jaw, Challenger exhaled sharply, "That man had the audacity—the sheer *nerve*—of claiming that his work was more important than mine!"

Cautiously stepping towards Professor Challenger, Diana drew a calming breath, "I am sorry, Professor...Drake is a difficult man under the best of circumstances. He is arrogant enough to believe that he can push people around through force of will. My only recourse in dealing with him is through asserting myself."

Rarely have I glimpsed such a sight at Challenger looking as pleased at someone as he did Diana at that moment. As his countenance grew more serious, he remarked, "I understand, dear child. He has also made some remarks about you as well...it is a shame that men like Drake do not understand how vast this world is and that the wonders of creation are as likely to be found in the natural world as they are in our fellow human beings."

As they smiled, I glanced at my pocket watch. It was nearing one o'clock, and I noted that we should take a lunch. Pointing behind me, Diana noted a pub with the large sign with the legend THE WORLD'S END.

Despite the sounds of yelling men emerging from behind the door of the pub, Challenger charged forward and swung the door open. Following him, I saw that many of the patrons were working men in the village. Despite their increasingly lower tones, the large, burly man with curly brown hair held the blade of his hunter's knife against Drake's throat. Despite that sight and the unwanted attention of the working men, Diana held firm as if familiar with such attention. All three of us stood as silent witnesses to what was transpiring.

"Shut yer bloody bone box," Scraping the blade against Drake's throat, the man spoke in veiled throats. "You butter on bacon types have no right comin' here and lookin' inta our business!"

"I'm...sorry for the insult," Drake mumbled, hoping to save face as he pleaded, "Listen, Mr. Scarver...I am sorry for the insult. However, my young assistant...from the East...might provide pleasant company..."

Storming forward, Challenger grabbed Scarver's arm and spun the man to face him. Dropping his knife, Scarver was surprised at Challenger's audacity. Looking Scarver in the eye, Challenger bellowed, "What is this insanity?"

Regaining some composure, Scarver poked Challenger's lapel as he spoke, "Listen, mate...I don't know what bloody podsnappery you and your friends are engagin' in...But your lot are *not* welcome here."

Straightening himself, Drake spoke with false Dutch courage, "We are welcome *wherever* we like! I would suggest you, Challenger, and the two other chattering monkeys go find a decent organ grinder."

As I tensed my fist, Diana grabbed my arm in an effort to hold me back. Glimpsing my mood, Challenger shook his head in an effort to dissuade me. Even Scarver took note, and he looked to be a man used to a physical challenge.

A cruel smile spread on Scarver's face like a cat discovering a plate of tuna, "I like you, *boy*...you know when to get into a good fight. The guy who pounded Hulke...provoked when he was told he owned the library twopence for a *library* book. At least you know a right pile of puddin' when you see it."

With the arrogance of someone who avoided the gallows, Drake asserted to Scarver, "And let me tell you that you uneducated ruffians in this...*quaint*... village have messed with the wrong individual. I will ensure that not only is this village to be avoided but that certain individuals will find themselves without work and prohibited from the finer halls of academia!"

Both Challenger and I noted how Diana pursed her lips as her brow furrowed. As arrogant as Challenger could be, he could not countenance threats directed at those who could not protect themselves. Moving Scarver aside, he glared at Drake with malevolence in his eyes. Despite his well-tailored suit and bushy beard, Challenger's aspect resembled a Neanderthal hunting a saber-tooth tiger.

Lowering his voice to a near-growl, Challenger warned, "Listen, Mr. Drake, as I shall *not* waste my breath a second time. We are both learned men who are here for important work. Make any threat against the three of us—Mr. Malone, Miss Chen, or myself—and I shall consider you my greatest enemy. My contacts extend within academia *and* His Majesty's government. Any effort to interfere with our work—or your assistant's—and I shall endeavor to destroy your already tenuous reputation, and ensure that the only history you teach will be in one of London's tawdriest private schools!"

A sharp exhale of breath revealed that Drake was admitting defeat. Without any words, he quickly turned and left the pub. Almost immediately the other customers resumed their drinking and revelry as if nothing had happened. Noting that Diana and I were shaken but otherwise fine, Challenger turned back towards Scarver.

Continuing his low, malevolent tone, Challenger addressed Scarver, "And *you* are the worst kind of bully, sir. Despite his obnoxious manner, Drake did not deserve physical threats. Might I remind you that you need to observe common decency?"

"Maybe that public school training works in hoity-toity London," Scarver snarled. "But 'ere...it's just puffery poofery. In *this* village, *we* don't appreciate high-and-mighty types tellin' us what to do or pokin' around our business. We *pride* ourselves on who we are, and we *don't* like others comin' in and placin' their noses where they don't belong..."

Placing the tip of the knife against Challenger's nose, Scarver cruelly smiled, "...because wankers like *that* get their noses chopped off. Understand?"

Sheathing his knife on his hip, Scarver grabbed a mug full of beer from the bar. Gulping it down, he slammed the mug on the bar and glared at Challenger. Confident that he had won some unspoken contest, Scarver strolled out of the bar. As he left, Challenger approached the pubkeeper—a man with long white hair, beard, and glasses who strongly resembled St. Nicholas in an apron—and ordered some food.

Despite all that had happened, the three of us made our way to a far table and ate in silence.

After lunch, Challenger and I worked on setting up equipment and taking measurements into the early part of the evening. Although Challenger's room provided the amenities for a makeshift observatory (complete with a portable telescope of significant power), our specialized equipment was located within a small shack behind the inn. Between large stacks of books and papers as well as Challenger's equipment, there was barely enough room for two people. With Drake's additional books and records taking considerable space, Challenger seemed particularly challenged to negotiate the shack with his considerable bulk. It had not helped that Oxford and the Royal Astronomical Society had meager resources for research and that Renswick Vale did not have the proper amenities, making our task extraordinarily challenging, to pardon the pun. The only benefit to this shack was its position. There were no mountains or hills to impede visual sight nor inclement weather to impede our equipment function. It was a perfect location to measure unusual readings from Halley's Comet. Challenger had installed the telescope within his room merely because there had been inadequate space for it in our small environs. Along one wall near a window lay the majority of our equipment: several boxes with switches and dials, another with an appendage that resembled a pie plate on its side. Flipping several switches, Challenger watched as a strip of paper with multicolored lines emerged from an even third box. Briefly, he glanced out of the window towards the afternoon. Examining the paper, Challenger looked at the dials and then towards me.

"That is *strange*," Challenger mumbled as he dropped the paper. "I had carefully refined the equipment to the correct settings. The dials show *no* interference and indicate normal settings. Halley's Comet is not fully visible, yet Madame Curie's equipment registers significant radio-activity."

"Wouldn't the sun provide some radio-activity?" I asked.

Contemplating a moment, Challenger postulated, "It would, but not at this degree. At least, that's what my colleagues at the Society indicated."

"But what is all this for, anyway?"

"Do not be dismiss me." Noting my boredom, Challenger pointed out every piece of equipment, "*That* is a high-level radio-activity detector. And the box with the round appendage is a Marconi-scope, invented by my colleague Lawrence, intended to detect radio-waves from celestial bodies. Now let's get on with it!"

As we refined the settings on his equipment, Challenger and I politely discussed the current theorems and ideas about the nature of comets and other celestial bodies. Much of those theories would take too long to relate in this narrative. Suffice it to say that both Challenger and I shared the idea that our cosmos was vaster, and more beautifully intricate, than our knowledge— or our imaginations—could conceive.

As the sky darkened, I felt my mood and temperament to become extremely peculiar. It was a kind of low-hanging ennui, a sense of impending dread that I could neither place nor justify. When I expressed these concerns to Challenger, he thought I might have inhaled particles from the large gray blankets that covered our equipment. The Royal Astronomical Society had paid a large amount to fund this scientific expedition, and I believed I could work through my discomfort to help Professor Challenger ensure exceptional results.

Finishing the first stage of our work, Challenger turned a variety of switches and dials which would activate the equipment before dawn. Making our way back to the inn, Challenger and I found our way to the dining room and enjoyed a cold collation. Through the walls, we could hear Drake and Diana conversing in the waiting-room of the inn. As their voices grew louder, Challenger and I had made our way to join them. Despite the assortment of chairs, a small sofa, and a fireplace, both of them were standing.

Bellowing with anger, Drake pointed at Diana, "You have done *nothing* but gossip with these...these townspeople! I have been working all day—"

"I am collecting the oral history of the village, Mr. Drake," As her face contorted into a scowl, Diana stood her ground. "I have been finding out—"

"Nothing but gossip and wasted time!" Spinning on his heels, Drake started to walk away. Upon seeing Challenger and myself, he turned back towards Diana and growled, "And you're worse than Challenger! You've spent more time flirting with his young associate than doing your job!"

Pushing his way past me, Challenger grabbed Drake's shoulder and spun the man around. As Drake faced him, Challenger bellowed in sarcasm, "First, my *dear sir*, Miss Chen is being more professional towards your rude and arrogant behavior than I can ever *hope* to be. You are also, Mr. Drake, a perfect exemplar of how high vocal volume negatively correlates with high intelligence. And as for your—"

"*Spare* me your pompous heroics, Professor Challenger," Seething with contempt, Drake spoke with renewed confidence. "You do not impress me, and as far as you should be concerned, you and Miss Chen are nothing more than obligations by His Majesty's government to keep our coffers filled!"

As his head straightened, Challenger's eyes took on a familiar tone. He was not a man to be trifled with, especially when he knew he had the moral high ground.

Inserting herself between Challenger and Drake, Diana asked, "Are you saying, Mr. Drake, that the *only* reason I am here is because of some...trade agreement?"

Taking a sharp intake of breath, Drake allowed a cruel smile on his lips, "That...and the fact that men like Mr. Malone have very...*exotic* tastes."

Something in Drake's manner cut me to the quick. It was one thing to besmirch my good name, or even Challenger's...but his own *assistant*? Even Challenger was struck at the man's seeming insanity as Diana stepped away. Both Challenger and I joined her in solidarity.

Possessed with hysteria, Drake snarled, "Get away from her! That raven-tressed Jezebel has done nothing but hinder my efforts! She must *pay!*"

Unaware of the growing sense of rage within me, I snarled, "You are nothing but a braggart and a coward, Drake! I *dare* you to test my mettle!"

As Diana rushed towards Challenger, Drake leaped and attempted to strike me. Although he missed, I managed to deliver a powerful right into his midsection. Stumbling backward, Drake glanced towards the fireplace. Although there were two swords and scabbards mounted above the fireplace in the inn's reception room, his attention turned towards the long, tall container which contained tools for handling the blazing fire.

Even in retrospect, I cannot place my feelings or actions into any rational context. Hostility and anger were flooding my thoughts without any primary cause. In other circumstances, some might say that I was possessed by spirits, yet I retain some memory of events. It was as if I was both participant and viewer of my own actions. However, my record of what transpired in Renswick Vale would be incomplete and unnecessarily deceptive without any acknowledgment.

Seeing the opportunity, Drake strode towards the cylinder. Despite both Challenger and Diana advising me to stay back, I charged towards Drake. Drawing a fireplace poker like a sword from its scabbard, Drake swung it wildly, hoping to connect. As he missed, Drake let his arm holding the poker hang freely on his side. Within moments, I leaped and struck him with a powerful right fist. Dropping the poker as his knees buckled, Drake left himself open as I delivered a mighty upward swing which connected to his chin. Hearing Drake's back thump against the wall, I crouched to pick up the poker.

The only clear fact I remember from that moment: the look of abject fear and rage on Drake's face as I held the pointed end of the poker against his throat.

Looking to one side, Drake snapped, "Challenger! Are you going to allow your lackey to hurt me?"

"I will *kill* you before I allow you to harm your assistant—or anyone else!" My words surprised me.

Turning back towards me, Drake unbottled his rage, "You don't have a choice...Your mentor is an overrated bag of heated gas, you are nothing but a glorified hack, and I have experienced nothing but aggravation from your new...*concubine.*"

My thoughts and emotions flooded with unending rage. Holding my ground, I felt my heart beating in my throat. All I wanted to do was to plunge the tip of the poker into Drake's neck. His arrogance, his condescension, his entire manner suggested that the only way to alleviate my increasing fury was to end him then and there...

"Ned!" Challenger's voice managed to break through.

Dropping the poker, I turned to see Challenger and Diana in a far corner. Both of them regarded me with concern, but Challenger's feelings were laced with slight disappointment. Diana, however, had a look of both compassion and fear, as if my rage and anger had been directed at *her*. Despite the clearing of my mind after the incident, I remain rather angry at myself for my lack of self-restraint.

Charging into the room was Constable Hinchcliffe with a large, bald man. "The innkeeper's wife reported an incident. Is this true?"

Before I could say anything, Challenger bellowed, "Listen, here! This Drake fellow has been *nothing* but a nuisance to us! In fact, he provoked Mr. Malone into—"

"That's all I need to know," Hinchcliffe declared. Gesturing at the bald man, Hinchcliffe stepped back. As the bald man grasped his arm, Drake shuddered in shock.

Approaching Hinchcliffe, Challenger spoke in a soft, booming voice, "Where are you taking him?"

"He will spend the night in our holding cell," Hinchcliffe explained. "After all, this is the fourth incident of people instigating fights since sundown..."

"Where were the others?" Challenger asked.

"One was at the World's End, another in front of the Beacon of Hope memorial, and a third at the chemist's."

"Is there any commonality between the incidents?" Challenger asked.

"Only if you consider good-hearted people becoming violent," Hinchcliffe pondered for a moment. "If there was a full moon outside..."

"Balderdash!"

"Still..." Looking at the three of us, Hinchcliffe concluded, "I would not plan to go outside tonight for *any* reason. Constable Burgess and I can handle things..."

As Hinchcliffe followed the bald man and Drake out of the inn, Challenger gathered me and Diana towards him. "I think there's more to this story than what Hinchcliffe was letting on..."

"Do you believe this is related to what happened yesterday?" Diana asked after briefly glancing at me.

Challenger pondered the question in silence. Despite his reputation for boisterousness and belligerence, George Edward Challenger had a peaceful, serene quality when contemplating a problem.

Scowling, Challenger muttered, "I believe so..."

Hoping to ensure my new colleague's safety I offered, "Perhaps Miss Chen could assist in recording our nightly observations?"

After a few tentative steps, Diana placed her hand on my shoulder. "I will head up to my room. I have various notes to organize and assemble, and it's been a rather long day for me. Good night, all."

Challenger addressed me as she left, "However, I *would* appreciate your assistance in recording my visual observations of the comet."

Sighing with resignation, I was hoping for the distraction of meaningless labor. Noticing my lack of interest, Challenger pointed as he confronted me in the now empty waiting room.

"Do not be so soppy!" Challenger bellowed. "That fool Drake received *precisely* what he had coming to him. Speaking of the two of us as he did... and that poor assistant of his...one day, men will realize that our differences strengthen our common nature. But until then..."

Breaking Challenger's concentration, I suggested, "But do you think what happened tonight is related to..."

"Three incidents since sunset? A savage beating by a meek and mild gentleman yesterday?" Grinning like a schoolboy, Challenger demonstrated great enthusiasm and curiosity. "Of *course* I believe they're related! Everything that has happened since we arrived at Renswick Vale is related! It is just a matter of finding the correct connections!"

Heading upstairs, I thought I heard a great clamor rise from outside. Dismissing them, Challenger chose to observe the comet from the solitude and silence of his room. Making my way to bed, my sleep was fitful and erratic.

Poking her head into the shack, Diana asked, "Did you hear what happened last night?"

As Challenger waved her inside, I regarded Diana in a more casual light. She had undone the tight bow of her hair, allowing it to flow on her shoulders. Hanging on a chain around her neck were her spectacles, and she had dressed in a plain brown dress. Regarding us with worry in her eyes, Diana seemed genuinely relieved that we were all right. She was a welcome break from our record-keeping and note-taking that morning. Only several loose wax paper wrappings indicated that Challenger and I enjoyed a brief lunch.

"One of the staff told me that there were *several* incidents last night," Diana related. "Men getting into physical altercations, at least one couple having a large row at the World's End..."

Keeping silent, I nodded my head. Challenger merely scowled at a long piece of paper coming from one of the machines in the room.

"Blast it!" He yelled, and then looked at us. "These levels of radio-activity are excessively high!"

"But wouldn't the comet emit such radiation?" I asked. "After all, that *is* why we're here—"

"Radio-activity is not instantaneous," Challenger explained. "Halley's comet is a considerable distance from this planet. In order to get these readings, it would have to be on top of us. And no, the sun would *not* account for this amount."

Pulling up the only other chair in the shack, Diana sat down. "Could Mr. Drake have—"

"No, he couldn't," Challenger interrupted. "Even if he came in the middle of the night, he would not know what switches to flip. Besides, I hope he enjoys his respite behind bars..."

"He will," despite her efforts towards a civil tone, the sarcasm and contempt in Diana's voice betrayed her. "He had managed to insult Constable Hinchcliffe *and* Scarver this morning."

"What happened?" I asked.

"Constable Burgess had arrested Scarver for instigating a fight," Taking a short glance at me, Diana continued, "Actually, the fight was already in progress and Scarver was—according to Burgess, anyway—telling them to 'kill each other.'"

"And Burgess threw Scarver in the same cell as Drake?" As his brow furrowed, Challenger contemplated the matter. "That does not sound—"

"Things were busy last night," Diana said. "Scarver was let out this morning after Drake referred to him as an 'inbred mongrel neanderthal.' Thanks to *that*, Hinchcliffe is allowing Drake to stay an extra night in jail."

"But what about your work?" I asked.

Clearing her throat, Diana sat up as she spoke, "See, that's the thing...now I can work unencumbered. Despite what Mr. Drake may say, history is not just a collection of documents and records. It's a *living*, breathing process..."

"And you've been collecting the spoken history of Renswick Vale." Allowing himself a broad grin, Challenger looked extremely impressed.

Returning Challenger's grin, Diana took great pride in her words. "Speaking with many of the elder residents, there are rumors and legends concerning periods of great upset. No one knows how or why...in fact, many of my mentors claim that these legends started with the witch trials in the early 17th century..."

Challenger harrumphed, "Witchcraft...Balderdash! Those incidents would have been in Drake's records! He would have known—"

"He *refused* to know, Professor Challenger." Leaning forward, Diana spoke with greater urgency. "Oxford had encouraged me to take the initiative since

"Go investigate the Beacon. Determine its composition."

Drake was more interested in gaining tenure and reputation than the truth. It was only through one of my initial conversations with a village elder that I learned of this. No one in living memory knows how or why these incidents happen...only that they occur with some regularity."

"Nothing has 'some' regularity, Miss Chen." Although postured to give a lecture, Challenger flashed a grim smile, "I have found that complexity and intricacy often underlie the most basic of mysteries. We appear to be experiencing another one of these incidents. We have already been placed on the chess-board; it is *imperative* that we see this gambit through to checkmate!"

"But how do we proceed?" I offered. "After all, we only—"

"Look at what we *do* know, my boy!" Seething with excitement, Challenger's voice rose in enthusiasm. "Men are attacking each other—unprovoked! You yourself have experienced this, Mr. Malone! All we need to do is determine the source..."

As his voice dropped off, Challenger pondered his equipment in a far corner. Returning his glance to the paper, he examined it before bellowing orders.

"Mr. Malone, Miss Chen," Professor Challenger bellowed. "Go investigate the Beacon. Determine its composition."

"But *you're* the scientist, Professor Challenger," Diana complained.

Before Professor Challenger could respond I asserted, "Neither Diana nor I are qualified...nor do we have the proper equipment..."

"But you do, Mr. Malone," Challenger countered. "You are both intelligent, observant, and capable of discerning the truth. At the very least, you can walk through the town with minimal disruption."

"And you will—?" I asked.

"I will stay here through the evening and work," Challenger stated. "After all, now that Drake will be incarcerated until tomorrow at the very least, I do not have to worry about his interference."

With that, Diana and I said our farewells and made our way through the village. I was reluctant to address her formally about the previous evening's events; shame and regret at my behavior the previous evening had inhibited any desire for personal disclosure.

Soon, we made our way to the Beacon of Hope. Standing as a silent sentinel, the large white monument appeared almost preternaturally clean amongst the everyday grime of Renswick Vale. As people made their way through the village, only a few of them regarded us with anything other than suspicion. Whether they believed that *we* were the ones bringing chaos into the Village or not, they provided no answer and I refuse to speculate.

Placing my palm against the cool white surface, I was surprised at the lack of grit. "I don't believe it's marble...perhaps it is the same composition as the

White Cliffs of Dover?"

As I stepped back, Diana remarked, "Those are made of chalk. Even *I* know that."

Seeing an opportunity, I turned towards Diana, "Look, I would like to apologize for my behavior last night. It was...unfortunate..."

"Do not worry," she responded with slight fear in her eyes. "I think...Mr. Drake has that effect on people."

Unsure of how to proceed, I merely kept quiet. After all, the ferocity of my actions the previous evening was enough to warrant some distrust on my colleague's part. My sole efforts to make amends would be in changed behavior rather than verbal apologies.

"It's funny," I countered. "Professor Summerlee—one of Challenger's colleagues—has a history of instigating arguments. When he does with Challenger, it is towards a particular point. But Drake..."

"Drake is full enough of himself to argue for its own sake." Irritation lined Diana's voice.

Taking a short pause, I asked Diana, "Didn't you mention something about this area being .."

Slightly taken aback, Diana countered, "I know there were some rumors in Roman times...but now I am wondering if all of this is connected."

"Perhaps it *is*," I suggested before a loud voice interrupted us.

"What're *you* still doin' 'ere?"

Both of us turned to see Scarver dragging a shovel behind him. His clothes and hands were caked with dirt, and his demeanor suggested a man in dire need of a drink.

Before we could protest, Scarver pointed and snarled. "You both *ain't* welcome here! Why don't you take the large pig with the poncy prince and leave? Nobody wants you here. *Nobody.*"

"Even if we could leave, we would need to arrange transportation," I asserted. "Even with a telegraph—supposing you *have* such a device—it would take an additional day or so."

Allowing the shovel to fall beside him, Scarver unsheathed his knife and aimed the tip for my throat. "Listen here, mate, know what I do for a livin'? I get my *hands* dirty...and I don't mind gettin' 'em *bloody* as well."

Despite the cruelty of his words, I remained relatively calm. As the sky began growing dark, I turned to see the Beacon starting to glow with a greenish tint. After I nudged her with my arm, Diana turned and witnessed the glow as well.

Grabbing my shoulder, Scarver turned me to face him and placed the blade on my throat. "When I talk to you, boy, you *better* listen. I don't want excuses or fairy stories, I want you to get outa this town!"

"Why should we listen to you?" Diana asserted.

"Because I know everything about this town," Scarver boldly claimed with the knife to my throat. "I know where the bleedin' *bodies* are buried!"

"Of course you would," a voice asserted. "You *are* the town's gravedigger, after all."

Approaching us was Constable Burgess, patrolling the village for signs of strife. Sheathing his knife, Scarver went to pick up the shovel.

"Not so fast, Scarver," Burgess' voice had a confident tone. "You're coming with me. A night in jail should do you a world of good."

"I ain't goin' *nowhere*," Scarver poked at Burgess' chest. "You don't have the *right* to take me in. I'm not doing anything."

"They're *guests*," Burgess countered.

"They're bloody *nuisances*. They've been the ones rilin' the town!"

Neither I nor Diana had an appropriate response.

"That's not your concern," Burgess replied.

"Everything's my concern. I know everything that happens in this town..."

"Perpendicular lunch talk as the Admiral of the Red at the World's End doesn't make you a smart man, Mr. Scarver." For a moment, Scarver tensed as if about to strike Burgess. However, he sprang with a great leap and ran through the village. Excusing himself, Burgess followed behind hoping to apprehend the man.

A small group of villagers had collected around us pointing and making comments. Rather than serve as the object of their attention, Diana and I made our way through the village to a small public garden. It was about as wide as an average sitting-room, with a large variety of flowers and small flora providing color. Except for a large bench along one side, this area was untouched by human influence. After asking Diana if she would join me, we made our way down a small path towards the bench.

Sitting at opposite ends, Diana and I took in the relative peace of the garden. We were both busy assisting others with their work, and we needed some respite and personal peace of our own. It was the closest we would come to privacy without locking ourselves in our rooms at the inn.

Allowing myself the luxury of a smile, I sighed and said, "This is...quite lovely."

"I know," Diana said. "Despite all that has happened the last few days..."

Her voice took on a heavier tone, and a sad feeling flashed on her face which matched the ever-darkening sky as the afternoon started changing into night. At that point, I was unsure of how to console her.

"You look bothered by something," Diana preempted me from addressing her.

Unsure of what to say, I offered, "I just...you have been through so much in the past few days."

Pursing her lips, various emotions flashed in Diana's eyes. Anger, guilt, sorrow...and I had no idea what to say to prove further comfort.

Frustration and anger tinged Diana's speech. "So much? What you might consider 'so much' is what I endure on a daily basis. Drake's contempt, Scarver's blatant malevolence, your angry outburst..."

Listening in silence, I felt somewhat ashamed. Although I wanted to defend my actions...I had no other rationale.

Although her manner was still, her voice was slightly tinged with anger, "I know you meant well...you were trying to protect me. But I know that every person, every place has a secret history—a hidden story never spoken aloud but whispered in shadows and secret corners. It is neither found in documents nor bound in volumes, but told by those who live in the aftermath."

"I...apologize for my behavior," I blurted out with great guilt.

"It is not just you," Diana countered. "I have been talking with many of the residents of Renswick Vale. They have recounted tales passed down from their forbears about times of great insanity and tumult. The witch trials were one such period, but there is no one in living memory who can recount the exact circumstances of these times."

Leaning forward, I listened with rapt attention and began to empathize with Diana. My own work as a chronicler of Challenger's exploits was based on fact refracted through my own perception. I had an objective fact in my favor: Diana faced a similar conflict.

"And Drake took issue with this?" I interrupted.

Scorn grew on Diana's face, "Yes, but not *just* because he prefers to rely solely on data. You've noticed how he has treated me with disrespect."

I nodded my head in assent. Diana continued, "He believes that he is... innately superior. He has read some of the drivel that paints the Chinese as some exotic evil. Many men believe that those not like them are less worthy of respect. I have seen how some of the men in this village regard me...and it is *not* pleasant."

Before I could apologize again, Diana interrupted, "And perhaps you have your own bias...after all, I have read of your recent heartache with Gladys. It reminded me of a young man I know...his name is Richard. He is a colleague of mine at Oxford, and I can tell by the look in his eyes that he is...infatuated with me."

"Does that bother you?" I asked.

Diana sighed, "Yes...and no. I am unsure if he sees me as a person or some 'perfumed grisette', as one of your tawdry keyhole journalist colleagues might say. He is sweet and pleasant, but I do not share his affections. Like this village, Richard has his own untold stories..."

Our conversation progressed and focused on a variety of other topics. For the first time during our mutual stay in Renswick Vale, I felt relaxed and calm. Although there was still some tension between us, Diana appeared more relaxed as dusk quickly approached. Although a slight sense of irritation spasmed through my body, I simply dismissed it as the oncoming chill of night.

At one point, Diana shushed me and gestured to listen. There was a low roar of anger serving as background noise, with the occasional grunts and sounds of metal clashing against each other. Women's anguished screams could be heard, and I rose from the park bench. Noting my posture, Diana rose and had a similar notion of escape.

Before we could run, we turned to hear a loud, guttural scream of rage. Turning, we saw a woodsman running towards us with a raised axe. His face was contorted in anger, and his eyes had a predatory look. Yet before we could run, we heard a loud bang that resulted in the man falling to the ground. His back had exploded, and blood covered his flannel shirt. In the distance was another, slimmer man aiming a shotgun in our direction.

Without hesitation, we both ran back into the village. Around us, men were attacking each other savagely, and corpses were already beginning to fall to the ground. Tapping me on the shoulder, Diana pointed towards a passageway and mouthed the word, *"Inn?"*

Nodding in assent, we made our way through various buildings, hoping to avoid the erupting carnage surrounding us. The only thing that interrupted our escape was discovering the Beacon of Hope in the center of the town.

As the night sky darkened, the Beacon stood as a frightening avatar of the chaos that surrounded us. Despite its normal whitish color, the Beacon had an eerie greenish-white glow in the ever darkening night sky. As we both glanced at the large white obelisk, I felt the familiar sensations of rage that had enveloped me the previous evening, but I held myself in check.

Just then, a voice yelled, "Kill them! Kill the strangers!"

A group of men wielding a variety of weapons followed Scarver, who was brandishing a sharpened hunting knife. Blocking our route towards the inn, Diana and I turned and ran through the streets. As we progressed, various men rushed from various alcoves and passageways. As Diana and I swiftly moved to avoid them, I found that these men were driven by an irrational, savage, and unwarranted rage. Although we managed to avoid direct attack, Diana and I found ourselves pursued by the men of Renswick Vale, the women and children presumably barricading themselves in their homes.

Evading our pursuers for the moment, Diana and I had come across the Library of Renswick Vale, its door closed but unlocked. Twisting the knob, Diana and I entered to find the library empty but recently vandalized. Hoping to find some comfort amongst the papers and torn volumes strewn across the floor, I attempted to move one of the smaller bookshelves to barricade the door. After Diana helped me drag the case in front of the door, we walked towards the back of the library to find appropriate shelter.

Making our way towards the rear of the library, we heard a loud *crash* from the front of the library, and Scarver's voice yelling, "Get them!" Running towards the back, Diana and I found an opened door and made our way inside.

As I locked the door behind me, I turned to Diana. She had been looking for a way to leave the isolated rear office. Anger reeked from the mutterings of the men outside who had been pursuing us. Our only illumination was light from the gas lamps outside filtered through a high window on a far wall. Neither Diana nor I had any ability to climb that high to emerge, and nothing in the cluttered office could serve as an appropriate stepping stool. As I swiftly approached Diana, I nearly tripped and fell onto my female companion. Regaining my footing, I looked down to see a slight gap in the wooden floor as the corner of a rug had been moved back. Moving the rug back, I saw that a trap door had been cut into the floor.

Putting a finger to my lips, I caught Diana's attention as I pointed to the floor. Handing me the office key in silence, she opened the trap door and descended down a small set of stairs. Noticing that I could latch the trap door from the inside, I began my descent after her. As I sensed a light turn on behind me, I closed the door and secured the latch.

Through the ceiling I heard Scarver's muffled yell, "Open the damn door! Yer both due fer slaughter!"

Within moments, we both heard a loud crash above followed by the rush of footsteps. Hoping that we would not be detected, Diana and I kept silent as we heard a variety of crashes, smashes, and bumps from above. Moved by some unknown force, the assorted throngs of Renswick Vale were in the midst of a bloodthirsty rage focused on me and my colleague. Placing her hand on my shoulder, Diana turned me to face her. She shared my sheer terror at how the people of Renswick Vale so quickly descended into barbarism.

We waited silently until the boisterous sounds from above started dissipating, and we kept silent for a few moments. Turning her head, Diana tapped me on the shoulder and I pointed around us. Our descent found us in a space slightly larger than a regular sleeping room. Along the far wall lay a wooden foldable cot—the kind of military cot that Sir John Roxton used in his expeditions. A small faucet and washbasin sat in a far corner beside it, and a pile of blankets stood beside that. Thankfully, Diana had lit a small oil lamp sitting on a battered desk. Open on the desk was a book, open with the date from two days ago written on the blank page. Beside it was a tied leather pouch, and a pen with open inkwell stood between both. On the opposite wall stood a bookcase lined with burgundy-covered bound volumes, each journal with the year embossed on the spine.

Remaining silent and vigilant, Diana and I waited until the savage footsteps ceased pounding on the ceiling. Hearing the primeval grunts from Scarver and his throng fade in the distance, Diana and I regarded each other with concern. Neither one of us seemed willing to venture forth from the secret room towards the streets of Renswick Vale. The tenor of the village had changed with swift rapidity from a quiet pastoral location into a bastion of terror.

Unnerved by the silence I whispered, "Did you notice the Beacon?"

Huddling towards me Diana responded in a whisper, "Yes! It glowed with a strange light."

Stepping towards me, Diana asserted, "We cannot leave until morning, you know..."

Our situation was rather precarious: the residents of Renswick Vale were under some primeval mesmeric influence and driven towards malice. Scarver's own misanthropy motivated him to seek out select targets, and he had fixated his homicidal intentions on Diana. Ignoring my own speculations on Scarver's motivations, I glanced at my pocket watch and noted the lateness of the hour.

Returning the watch to my waistcoat pocket, I listened for any remaining noise from upstairs. Hearing none, I spoke with Diana in a soft voice, "It *is* rather late, and although it may seem inappropriate, perhaps we should spend the night here. We could easily sleep in shifts..."

Pulling up the chair, Diana sat at the desk. Even in the flickering oil lamp, I could see a look of curiosity play upon her face. Opening the leather pouch, she withdrew some faded, aged sheets of paper and spread them out across the desk.

Turning back towards me, Diana looked at me with concern. With some trepidation, she stammered, "That would be a good idea...I don't..."

Removing my watch from its waistcoat pocket, I placed it upon the desk near her. Stepping back, I raised my palms, "Do not be concerned...I will do *nothing* untoward nor will I dishonor you or sully your reputation. My behavior towards you will remain proper, appropriate, and courteous."

As the light from the oil lamp flickered, Diana's face had a rather melancholic look. She whispered, "I believe you, Ned. In fact, I would like to examine these records...if only to satisfy Mr. Drake's curiosity. Besides, you are probably tired...and concerned about Professor Challenger."

Zounds! In the midst of recent chaos, I had completely forgotten about Challenger. Despite my faith in his ability to handle himself, I must admit to some concern about leaving Challenger alone with his equipment. My concerns and feelings were not alleviated by the malevolent air that encompassed Renswick Vale.

My voice feigned unwarranted courage. "As much as I would like to check on Challenger, I would dare not venture out and leave you unguarded."

My efforts to sound confident must have impressed Diana, for she flashed a slight grin. "Good. These papers may be nothing more than trifles, but I believe they are worth investigating...especially given Hulke's position as town record keeper."

Slowly, my cognition returned as I remembered the events of the last few days: the assault on Roderick Hulke, the initial wave of chaos, and my own attack on Drake. Honestly, I was surprised by Diana's trust in me. Perhaps she was willing to have me nearby because she did *not* trust me, but I was in no position to argue.

After asking Diana to wake me within two hours, I went towards the cot. Folding my jacket into a crude pillow, I placed it at one end as I walked towards the washbasin. Removing a relatively clean blanket from the pile, I noticed my colleague glaring at the pages with some interest. As her face softened, Diana examined one of the pages in detail as I lay down in the cot. Covering myself with the blanket, I felt grateful that she and I were developing a bond. Although my bond with Challenger is cordial, there my bond with Diana was forged and strengthened through a sense of adventure. Even in the midst of our current crisis, we somehow were developing an easy familiarity.

"Take care," she said before opening the journal. "And good night."

"Good night," I responded, falling asleep quickly.

My next memory was hearing a rooster crow in the distance. Sitting up in the cot, I noticed Diana lifting her head from the desk. She had presumably fallen into slumber during the night, her eyes reflecting her tired state. Whether she intended to wake me or had fallen prey to her fatigue I will never know.

Rising, I unfolded my jacket and wrapped it over my arm. Placing a finger to her lips, Diana crooked her head to listen but found only silence. Making my way past her, I went up the small stairs and unlatched the trap door. Emerging through the trap door, I entered an office covered with bits of debris, torn papers and books, and splintered wood where a door once existed.

"Can you take these?" Diana asked from the room. Taking the journal and pouch from her, I stepped back as she made her way up the stairs. Closing the trap door, I escorted Diana through the library where the debris from torn volumes and smashed bookcases resembled starfish scattered along a foreign shore. A few brave souls had ventured inside the library to determine the extent of the damage and remained silent as we left. Whether they were part of the throng last night I am unsure, but was unwilling to seek confirmation.

Making our way outside, Diana and I found that Renswick Vale had descended into desolation and despair. Many buildings that were sturdy and strong the day before were now damaged and broken due to heavy vandalism. Burnt wood and loose stones stood where the World's End had welcomed thirsty patrons. A fair-haired woman regarded her tall, lanky husband in suspicion as he attempted an apology for unspoken acts. A four-year-old boy in his bedclothes was pointing towards a house, crying that his mummy would not wake up. Weapons of various kinds—clubs, knives, and guns—could be found lying at random points on the ground.

Tugging at my arm, Diana pointed towards the beacon. When I turned towards the Beacon of Hope, my heart sank as I saw that the normally white stone was liberally stained with drying blood. On the ground in front of the Beacon lay the corpse of Constable Burgess. A large gash crossed his neck, and the front of his shirt had a dark stain extending from his shoulders to the top of his belt.

"Mr. Malone! Miss Chen!"

Challenger was rushing towards us, carrying a large bundle wrapped in one of the protective blankets for our equipment. He appeared disheveled but otherwise unharmed.

"Professor!" I called out as he approached closer to us. "Are you all right—?"

"Quite so, my boy!" After regarding Diana with appreciative delight, he addressed me. "Our readings are through the..."

Noting the carnage surrounding us in the village, Challenger looked with great disgust. As I took the package from his arms, he looked around and then regarded us. "Are the two of you all right?"

"We're all right, Professor," I remarked. "But there's something you should..."

Storming towards the inn, Challenger yelled, "Come! We have much to do!"

Challenger was rushing towards them...

"But Professor!" Diana's voice could barely be heard amongst the cacophonous anguish, "Shouldn't we help!"

Spinning on the balls of his feet, Challenger addressed Diana for the first and only time during that period with some derision, "My dear, let Hinchcliffe handle this...this jiggery-pokery. We have more important scientific matters to discuss!"

We both followed Challenger back to the inn, with me carrying his package and Diana carrying the journals from the library. After leaving the Professor with his package at the inn's dining room, Diana and I went to our rooms to prepare for the day. As I managed to clean and dress, I could hear Challenger's voice booming at the innkeeper to prepare us a late breakfast. Making my way downstairs, I helped Challenger lay out various papers on the table as Diana made her way into the dining area. As I made space on the table, she laid out papers from the leather pouch and placed the now opened journal next to it.

Moving around the table towards us, Challenger pointed to the long strips of paper with colored lines. "The data was received was fascinating! Our equipment picked up a huge amount of radio-activity from Halley's comet."

"But isn't that what we were looking for, Professor?" I asked.

Pausing a moment, Challenger lowered his voice, "But *not* like this. You see...the levels recorded on these strips are too high; they should only be slightly higher than our normal readings. And one of my measuring devices nearly exploded."

"But last night, Professor..." interrupting Challenger was never a smart move, but I was growing impatient. "...we were attacked by men in the village—weren't you..."

"I was too busy working to be bothered by the commotion," Challenger dismissed me in a gruff tone. "I simply locked myself in our room and used the protective blankets to keep myself..."

Nudging Challenger's arm, Diana spoke with great resentment. "Ned and I were *trapped* in the library, chased down by Scarver and his miscreants. We ..."

Several chambermaids came in with platters of food, including muffins, pastries, and an assortment of fruit. Another carried a tray containing a pot of hot coffee, three cups, a small pitcher of cream and a small sugar bowl with a spoon. As Diana and I made room for the food on the table, Challenger merely glowered. Grabbing one of the pastries, Challenger consumed it in three large bites before pouring himself a cup of coffee.

As he gulped his coffee, I assembled a plate of food and poured myself a cup of coffee. Diana followed, opting to assemble a plate of fruit as I sipped my coffee and placed my food on the table. As Challenger placed his now-empty cup on the table, I related the previous evening's events. When I described the eerie greenish-white glow of the Beacon of Hope, Challenger sparked to life.

Rushing to examine the charts, he muttered to himself and then addressed the two of us.

While Diana and I stood and ate, Challenger's voice lifted as a devilish grin spread on his face, "Why, yes, of course....that would explain it!"

"Explain what?" I asked.

"The Beacon, my boy, the Beacon of Hope!" Twisting his gaze towards Diana, Challenger asked, "Miss Chen, you quoted a letter from John Renswick...what did you say led the Catholic settlers here?"

She answered without hesitation, "...*And we came across a shower of light raining on a beacon of hope*...but that doesn't fit, Professor Challenger."

"Doesn't fit?" Challenger scowled.

"The rock that was carved into the Beacon of Hope has been here since at least Roman times," Diana explained before eating a grape.

"But my dear...I mean, Miss Chen," Rare was the time when Professor Challenger would correct himself. "That makes sense...the Beacon of Hope may have been some unearthly debris which fell upon this planet centuries ago! That 'shower of light' may have been a preternatural manifestation of some other cosmic phenomena."

Rushing towards the pouch and journal, Diana reviewed some papers before looking up, "Professor, you may be correct...I found this journal documenting the years in which there was great unrest in Renswick Vale. I find that they correspond to a cycle of approximately seventy-six years starting in 1535, which is the founding of the village."

"So you're suggesting that the Beacon may be a kind of...divining rod for Halley's Comet?" I asked. The higher sciences were not in my field of expertise.

In an irritated tone, Challenger lectured. "Perhaps something Summerlee once told me could help you comprehend this phenomenon. One of his colleagues at the Royal Astronomical Society theorized that the tail of a comet was not debris, but the refraction of sunlight as the comet traveled through our solar system. That sunlight gives off unique radiation that hits our planet, and that the Beacon intensifies..."

"Like sunlight through a spyglass?" Diana asked with confidence.

"Precisely!" Shooting Diana a confident look, Challenger asked, "And would it be irrational to suggest that the witch trials took place during the comet's presence?"

"It would not," Diana was assured. "In fact, this journal—separate from the other materials in the library's hidden room—contains detailed descriptions of deaths, accidents, and other phenomena which occurred during these times. According to these entries, the librarian's job was to record this history so that there was a record, but *not* to make these issues public."

"Makes sense," I concluded. "After all, a community suffering religious persecution would *not* want tales of insanity and madness spread throughout England."

"And I theorize that the enhanced radio-activity from the comet enrages men with a solid target for their anger," Challenger scolded. "Hence your near-attack on Drake last night."

Hoping to escape embarrassment, I asked, "Then why didn't it affect you or Diana? Is it something in her female temperament?"

As Diana regarded me with slight contempt, Challenger responded. "Most likely, it is because Diana has had to shield her own anger at being mistreated by her fellow countrymen as a result of her heritage...a sad affair from which there is no easy tonic."

Diana gave Challenger a faint nod as if he understood. As far as Challenger himself, he remained silent, but I believed that his overall aggressive manner provided a barrier. However, confirmation would remain elusive.

Scratching his bearded right cheek, Challenger appeared lost in thought. Within moments, he regarded us with a sparkle of enthusiasm in his eyes. "Mr. Malone, Miss Chen....we will need to test the beacon for radio-activity."

"But how?" Diana asked.

"I think I have the right materials upstairs to perform a field test," Challenger muttered. "It will mean taking some chips from the Beacon....and we must make haste. Tonight is the last night that the comet will be prevalent in the sky...and tomorrow our transport back to London will arrive."

Seeing the worried look on her face, Challenger approached her and placed a fatherly hand on her shoulder, "Don't worry, Miss Chen...we will help you get back to London as well."

A sad grin spread on Diana's face as Challenger rushed me out of the room, barking, "Come, Mr. Malone, we have materials to collect!"

Kneeling at the base of the Beacon of Hope, I had placed the hammer and chisel on the ground. Next to me knelt Challenger, who grabbed a chunk of white stone from the ground. As he turned to Diana, she held a test tube full of clear white liquid. Beside her was a small pouch filled with vials of various substances. We were able to work undisturbed as the village residents worked towards cleaning up the debris and despair of the previous night's events. Thankfully, Burgess' corpse had been removed, leaving only a dark stain on the ground.

Dropping the stone into the test tube, Challenger asked, "Now you *did* mix the proper amounts of each chemical, didn't you, Diana?"

As her lips pursed in anger, Diana gave a small resentful nod. Before our eyes, purple-colored strands emerged from the rock and turned the liquid a dark purple color.

"Yes!" Challenger shouted. "My theory is right! The Beacon of Hope has residual radio-activity!"

Placing the test tube in one of the empty segments of the pouch, Diana closed it and placed the strap around her shoulder. All three of us rose as I picked up the hammer and chisel. Challenger had briefly explained the test—certain kinds of extreme radio-activity reacted with certain chemical agents when mixed together. I did not think to document the exact mixture, but the events in Renswick Vale served as a cautionary reminder that some things must remain secret.

"So what do we do now, Professor?" I asked.

"Unfortunately, there is no way for us to contact His Majesty's Government," Challenger responded. "However, I think one course of action—for tonight—is to cover as much of the Beacon as possible with our equipment coverings."

"Would it be wiser to keep the Beacon uncovered to see if it reacts again?" Diana asked.

Challenger's response was a blunt, "No. The Beacon acts as an amplifier for the sunlight and other radio-activity radiated through the comet. We cannot get accurate results, and our equipment might not stand a second attempt."

It was one of the few times I had seen Challenger sigh in defeat. Our sole purpose in visiting Renswick Vale was to have an unimpeded, direct path to measuring the strange energies and emanations of Halley's Comet. As the three of us stood in the town square, Constable Hinchcliffe strode quickly towards us. The look on his face did not suggest that all was well.

"I'm...sorry," Hinchcliffe lowered his face. "Mr. Drake is dead. Murdered in his cell last night."

My head snapped in shock at Hinchcliffe's words given the savagery of the previous night's assault. Diana's gaze wavered between Hinchcliffe and myself, unsure whether to pity or fear me. Only Challenger seemed unperturbed by the news; in fact, his face grew more pensive, and his voice sounded near-clinical as he spoke.

"What about the other prisoners?" Challenger asked. "Hadn't you appre-hended Scarver?"

Shame and recrimination reverberated in Hinchcliffe's voice. "We had, but his corpse was nowhere to be found. Both Drake and the other prisoner were badly beaten. We...I believe that Scarver was dragged off—"

"He was not," I asserted. "He led a group of men after us last night, thanks to the Beacon!"

Before Hinchcliffe could protest, Diana and I outlined the events of the previous evening, and Challenger expounded his theory about the Beacon's otherworldly origins. Raising his eyebrows slightly at our words, Hinchcliffe did little to disavow our theory.

"What do we need to do?" Hinchcliffe asked, shifting his focus to the villagers helping each other in the midst of the carnage.

"We must drape the Beacon in those coverings!" Pointing to a pile by the Beacon, Challenger's tone was assertive and belligerent. "Unless we prevent the radiation from seeping through, Renswick Vale will suffer a final night of ..."

"Nothing....unless you walk away from that mutton shunter and leave this village."

Taking aim at Challenger with his rifle, Scarver approached very slowly as a group of men followed him. His clothes were covered with blood, and his knuckles bore large red scrapes.

"You don't belong here," Scarver snarled. "You brought this chaos...you, your young friend, Drake and his lotus blossom!"

Clenching her fist, Diana struggled to maintain her composure. With my temperament in a questionable state, I nodded her off. Only Challenger seemed oblivious to Scarver's threat, stepping towards him with an executioner's confidence.

"My name is George Challenger, Mr. Scarver," The professor's voice was clipped. "Your Brunswick rifle is a bit long in the tooth...I assume it was your grandfather's?"

"My father left me this rifle," Scarver's voice grew cold. "He brought it with him after he served in China."

Challenger interrupted, "That explains your animosity towards Miss Chen, but tell me, Mr. Scarver... tell me what drives you to such desperate measures other than your father's work to ensure a steady supply of tea and opium."

Keeping his aim, Scarver pulled back the hammer of the rifle. "You don't understand, do you, Challenger? This village has been kept safe from outsiders for *years* thanks to our reputation. We stay because we need to stay apart from the chaos of the world. We don't need interlopers like *you* coming in and disturbing us..."

Stepping forward, Hinchcliffe started to bolt but backed down when Scarver aimed the rifle at him.

"Don't, constable...I'm more than happy to shoot *you*." Raising his voice, Scarver addressed the gathering crowd. "And it'll be as easy as slittin' Burgess' throat. "

As the crowd backed down, Scarver drew back a moment. Relaxing his aim, Scarver looked at the four of us with contempt and anger.

"You lot look down on people like me," Scarver snarled. "You think you're so bloody clever, don't you? Comin' here with yer young upstarts and your laundry washers bringin' chaos to our village...you lot were *never* welcome here. You'd think that you woulda stayed away with the stories..."

"You know as well as I, Mr. Scarver, that those stories are *not* true." Challenger mocked Scarver; the Professor did not suffer fools gladly.

Swiftly stepping back, Scarver aimed the rifle at Challenger as he countered. "Not so fast. Yer not gonna get the jump on *me*! After all, the only reason your nancy boy and his concubine are still breathin' is that they found Hulke's secret room..."

"You...knew about that?" Diana asked surprised.

As the rifle barrel took a swift arc towards Diana, Scarver said, "Of *course* I did! I told you that I knew everything that happens in town."

"Because you were training to be Hulke's replacement, weren't you?" I asked. Taking a quick glance at Hinchcliffe, he nodded as well.

Oblivious to both of us, Scarver stepped forward. Backing towards the Beacon, he looked around but could not find an easy escape. None of the villagers stepped forward

"Yeah, I was," Scarver snarled. "Everyone in this town looked down on me 'cause I got my hands dirty. Didn't have much schoolin'. Father was never quite right when he came back from China. But I was *smart*—smart enough to snoop when Hulke had me work on the library. Found the room, blackmailed the truth outta him..."

"...and bulled the people of this village into submission!" As he spoke, Challenger took a long stride.

As Diana backed into the beacon, Scarver caught Challenger out of the corner of her eye, "Back off, Challenger, or I'll shoot this bloody Mongol!"

Despite the fearful situation, Diana spoke with resolve. "Men like you and your father drove my grandparents out of China to England. Their village was destroyed, their neighbors were slaughtered, and their lives were ruined."

"Listen, girl..." Blind rage spread on Scarver's face. "...my father served England...and for what? Dying because he made long trips to London to visit Limehouse and its opium dens? Wanting to relive his glory days? *Your* people drove *my* father to despair and this village never respected my father. I'll *take* their respect with the back of my hand, the blade of my knife, or the barrel of a gun."

"Then why not shoot me first?" Challenger asked.

Deftly inserting himself between Scarver and Diana, Challenger glanced at me. As he mouthed *no*, I glanced at Hinchcliffe. He nodded in assent, and we both silently agreed on a course of action. As surprise registered on Scarver's face, we both regarded Challenger then nodded at each other. With the villagers paralyzed either with fear or the emanations of the Beacon, both of us had only one chance to succeed.

Facing Scarver, Challenger asserted, "After all, it was mere child's play for a blackguard like yourself. You read the secret history, discerned that the Beacon only affected men with strong resentments towards specific men, and acted accordingly. You were immune due to your resentment towards the entire village and your perceived persecutions, styling yourself as the village Napoleon and ruling through innuendo and intimidation."

Maintaining his aim, Scarver yelled, "Don't insult me...your friend Drake received a thorough beating when he shared a cell with me. You are at the wrong end of this rifle, Challenger. I *will* shoot you."

"Of *course* you will!" Even in the midst of physical danger, Challenger maintained a high level of belligerence and arrogance. "Why not shoot me in the face? Or the chest? Come on, man, show the kind of high-level backbone that your father showed in China."

Tensing his finger on the trigger, Scarver tightened his grip on the stock of the rifle. Noting an opportunity to escape, Diana slid out from between Challenger and the Beacon. Before Scarver could protest, Challenger mocked, "If you are anything like your father, you are nothing more than a pigeon-livered meater looking for an escape route. He probably went to London to escape your haggish mother and your petulant behavior."

"Do *not* insult me!" Scarver's voice grew loud and harsh. "I will kill you where you stand!"

Staring down the barrel of the gun did not intimidate Challenger; I almost suspect that he felt invigorated by the potential danger.

Squinting his eyes, Challenger regarded Scarver with contempt. "I doubt it, good sir. You are nothing more than a coward and a bully. You are nothing more than a klazomaniac who believes himself more sinned against than sinning."

Moving the barrel down towards Challenger's heart, Scarver's face grew more bestial in appearance. "Don't mock me! I *will* shoot you where you stand."

Both Hinchcliffe and I regarded each other in silence after noticing that Diana had made her way near me. She gestured that I take action, but I mouthed *no*. It was not a lack of courage on my part so much as a wish to avoid any unnecessary blood. Regardless of whether Challenger's confidence was valid or counterfeit, he stared down at the barrel of Scarver's rifle without flinching. Despite his reputation for being bellicose, Challenger could be reasonable if somewhat unpleasant in manner. At this moment, Challenger acted only to stop Scarver and avoid unnecessary bloodshed.

There was an audible gasp as Challenger said, "No, you won't. You act the same way many other men like you will in challenging situations: you will soil yourself and cry like a pathetic schoolboy punished by his mummy for misbehaving!"

Scarver's posture tightened and his finger began squeezing the trigger of the rifle. Both Hinchcliffe and I rushed towards Scarver, only taking two steps before reaching him. As Hinchcliffe grabbed the rifle out of Scarver's hands, I wrestled him to the ground. Kneeling over the man, I reached into the sheath on the side of his belt and removed his knife. Throwing it towards Hinchcliffe, I returned my attention to Scarver. I struck him in the face, knocking him cold.

As I rose from Scarver's body, I walked back towards Challenger, Diana, and Hinchcliffe. We merely regarded each other with concern as the crowd dissipated, either through deferred bloodlust or the aftereffects of the Beacon.

Holding the rifle in his hands, Hinchcliffe asked, "Do you know where the knife is?"

"Right here!" Diana held the knife with caution.

Holding the rifle in one hand, Hinchcliffe took the knife. All three of us turned to see several men walking Scarver away.

"Do not worry," Hinchcliffe said. "They are *my* men, taking Scarver back to prison."

"That is fine," Challenger's voice sounded slightly bitter. "The three of us will cover the Beacon with these coverings."

"Let me take these back to the constabulary," Hinchcliffe held up both items. "I will assemble some other villagers to help."

With that, Hinchcliffe left the three of us alone.

In the relative silence, Challenger said, "Thankfully, our escort back to London will be here in the morning, and we'll make arrangements with the Society to take care of the Beacon."

"What would they..." I began to ask.

Challenger interrupted. "If they were as clever as they believe themselves to be, they would extract this rock from the ground, send it on a ship and drop it into the deepest ocean. Otherwise, they will most likely ask the Corps of Engineers to remove it and place it in a Ministry archive."

"And the residents of the village?"

Challenger paused for a moment. "Their history will be written and...well, Miss Chen, what *will* happen?"

"I do not know." Diana's voice contained deep sadness. "After all, with Drake dead I would be responsible for writing the history, but after that...I don't know what my role will be..."

"First, young lady," Challenger regarded her with confidence. "I will speak with my contacts—I believe Summerlee has some pull. We should be able to find you another mentor to help you write the history."

Something in Diana's voice suggested distrust. "But what about after that?"

"Then, my dear," Challenger placed an avuncular hand on her shoulder, "I would be more than happy to hire you as one of my consultants. You have demonstrated great courage and initiative, and quite honestly, I have found you...refreshing."

As Challenger regarded me with some derision, Diana merely flashed a sad grin.

"However, Renswick Vale *will* lose its anonymity," Challenger said. "After the larger details are revealed, and they *have* to be revealed, the village can no longer depend on isolation for its survival. Their history, like all of human history, contains moments of inhumanity and disregard. Although exacerbated by more celestial phenomena, the violence and aggression of Renswick Vale are all too familiar...and the lessons learned here should *never* be forgotten."

THE END

The Secret History of a Pulp Character

Imagine you're a successful writer and your success is not based on the historical novels you tend to write, but a series of stories involving a character who's more of a distraction. You have three choices: you either give up and rest on your laurels, focus on writing the historical novels that have no audience, or create a unique new character and hope that lightning strikes twice.

Sir Arthur Conan Doyle took the third option in 1912 by creating Professor George Challenger in *The Lost World*. Although written as a tribute to H. Rider Haggard, *The Lost World* became what we now know as a "trope namer", and Conan Doyle created his second-best known character. Although Conan Doyle wrote two more novels and two short stories around the character, Professor Challenger never really took off in the same manner as Sherlock Holmes.

That's a shame because although he was reaching for an H.G. Wells-type style in his post *Lost World* Challenger stories, Arthur Conan Doyle created a character who could easily be the prototype for later characters like Bernard Quatermass and Doctor Who. (Don't argue that it's *"The Doctor"*-you know who I mean). Challenger seems ripe for further exploration—a "consulting scientist" in the early 20th century with its increasing interest in the sciences. I'll admit that I love finding public domain characters (if they are relatively obscure) and bringing out qualities that appeal to modern readers.

Some of my earliest work involved a comic around Wonder Man, a one-shot Superman riff, and I've worked on characters like Marty Quade (for Airship 27) and Doctor Nikola. So when I kept seeing PROFESSOR CHALLENGER as a character Airship 27 wanted to use, well...I started on my way. First off, reading all of the Challenger works via Delphi Classics' Conan Doyle Collection (http://www.delphiclassics.com) and various websites (the two short stories are not public domain in the US). Without much hyperbole, *The Lost World* and *The Poison Belt* are the best non-Holmes Conan Doyle works (and I'll fight you on those). You can skip *The Land of Mist*—not for its pro-Spiritualism stance but for the poor writing. But his two Challenger short stories—"When the Word Screamed" and "The Disintegration Machine"—redeem the character and are pretty solid reads.

After "research", I crafted a bible complete with links to places to download and/or read four out of the five Challenger works. It was easy to categorize the kinds of stories that Challenger would face: lost world tales, *Doctor Who/*

Quatermass-styled science fiction, and a "hidden years" between *The Poison Belt* and "When the World Screamed". Conan Doyle's writing decreased during World War One, and with over ten years between Challenger stories... why not assume that Challenger had other adventures? (Plus, pre-World War One England seemed fertile for exploration) In fact, it would give me an opportunity to write a Conan Doyle character without writing a Sherlock Holmes tale. I read enough Holmes pastiches for *I Hear of Sherlock* (http://www.ihearofsherlock.com) to know that I might subconsciously plagiarize another's tale, but with Challenger crafting an "original" story would be easy.

In fact, "The Secret of Renswick Vale" came from a pitch to Big Finish Productions for a Fourth Doctor audio. The pitch was rejected, but there was enough of a story to consider pitching it by replacing the Doctor with Challenger. However, explaining the premise would require Challenger to have knowledge outside of his native time, so I recrafted the story and set it in a remote English village. Further research into Halley's Comet gave me a year, as well as another story element. Given the nature of the story, I created a character who was a woman of color to provide a different perspective and highlight one of the themes. (I also took the liberty of "casting" John Rhys-Davies as Challenger, and when I thought of a man named "Drake" in a "Village"...well, think Patrick McGoohan). This story allowed me to indulge my adolescent love of British science fiction—so much so that the high-concept pitch for this story would be "Phillip Hinchcliffe produces the John Wyndham and Nigel Kneale scripted mashup of *Quatermass and the Pit* and *The Wicker Man*".

(If you know all of the people who I've referenced, e-mail me at gordon.dymowski@gmail.com and you'll win...a thank you note).

If you haven't already, check out the other stories in this collection. Then read Conan Doyle's Challenger stories. (Even if you have already read *The Lost World*, check out *The Poison Belt*). When you're finished, you'll understand why Professor Challenger is a great "hidden" character...and you'll want more.

Thanks for reading!

Gordon Dymowski has always had a hand in writing—everything from his childhood scribbling to writing a column for the **Loyola Phoenix**. (One of his prized possessions: a rejection letter for a spec **Columbo** treatment in the 1990s) By day, he provides marketing and copywriting services for non-profits and small businesses. At night, Gordon writes for a variety of outlets, including **I Hear of Sherlock, Chicago Now** and **Blog *This*, Pal** (http://blogthispal.

blogspot.com) Gordon's works have been featured in Pro Se Productions, Airship 27 Productions (including **Legends of New Pulp Fiction** and **Black Bat Mystery Volume 3**), and Space Buggy Press. For Gordon's online portfolio and contact information, please visit http://www.gordondymowski.com; you can purchase his works via Amazon at http://bit.ly/GDymAuthor

THE DESERT OF THE LOST

By Barbara Doran

When one travels with a man as given to expressing his opinions as Professor George Edward Challenger, one must expect to find him doing so on no uncertain terms. Indeed, from London to the fabled city of Kashgar, not a day had gone by without some argument or other between the good Professor and some unfortunate traveler too foolish to leave well enough alone.

If not for our patroness, of a sort, the good Professor would surely have seen the inside of various local holding cells on frequent occasions. Lady Francis Dennistoun, however, had an invaluable combination of tact and money with which to ease our passage.

She also had a talent for evading trouble by redirecting us around the worst dangers. Which, given her actual employment, should come as no surprise. An adventuress secretly working for His Majesty's Government must surely have frequent occasions to require such skills.

Her ladyship and I were just returned from Kashgar's marketplace, where we'd purchased supplies and a rather unpleasant looking cart for the next stage of our travels, when we heard the unmistakable bellow of my friend inside the hotel where we were staying.

"HOW DARE YOU, SIR!?"

Another voice piped up, softer but still carrying because its owner had to speak up to be heard. "Now my dear man, might I trouble you to be listening to all I'm having t'say afore leaping to conclusions." The Scots accent wasn't entirely unexpected. Kashgar was a central meeting place between East and West and there were travelers from all over staying in the same hotel.

A crash followed, along with another shout from my good friend Challenger. "STAND STILL, YOU LITTLE SNEAK!"

"Now, sir, if I were to be doing that you'd be breaking me in a heartbeat. T'is nae great fondness I have for being injured and I'd be nae use at all for weeks after."

The speaker sounded oddly cheerful, given he was likely the target of both Professor Challenger's ire and his fists. It made me curious as to what, exactly, was going on inside and I hurried up the steps. Lady Francis was just a touch faster, mostly because she'd begun moving as soon as she'd heard the Professor shout.

The lobby of the Gold Peony Hotel was somewhat damaged by the time we entered. To my surprise, the worst of it came from an overturned table and a chair that'd been tossed to the side. The fight itself was at the center of the room, between Professor Challenger and an oddly dressed young man.

At first glance the youngster might have seemed native. His clothes were a peculiar mix of European, Turkish and Chinese and his features were obscured by a newsboy cap and tinted glasses. Yet his accent was pure Scots and his hair was so blonde it was practically white. A traveler from our homeland who'd gone native, perhaps?

Given the stranger would barely make half myself, much less a man the girth of Professor Challenger, I could hardly blame him for keeping out of my friend's grip. He'd have done better, I thought, to make a quick exit. Fast as he was, he'd have escaped quite handily.

"Good show, boy. You teach the old bastard what's for." That came from the fourth in our little party, Captain Wright, late of His Majesty's Army and the one in charge of keeping us safe as we traveled. A thin dour-faced man, the Captain and Professor Challenger had little fondness for each other. Indeed, I suspect Captain Wright would happily be arguing and fighting with my friend himself if Lady Francis hadn't forbad it.

Seeing Captain Wright doing nothing whatsoever to stop the fight, Lady Francis stepped forward and said in a disappointed way, "Professor Challenger, you promised."

"Well, and I did, my dear. But you can hardly expect me to stand for my reputation being impugned. And by an upstart student of McKenzie's at that!" Nevertheless, Professor Challenger lowered his hands, his tempest quelled in moments.

The young man, seeing he was safe, relaxed a little. "Now, Professor, if you were to be listening to all I said, instead of leaping on a fellow afore he'd a chance to finish, you'd know I did nothing of th'sort."

Professor Challenger glared. "And what, exactly, am I supposed to take from your claim the things we learned from South America were a hoax?"

"Nae, sir. Twas ne'er my intent to be saying that and it's sorry I am you think I did." The youth straightened his clothes. "I was saying I'm thinking it's impossible for the things you found to persist several score million years without changing."

Professor Challenger's fists clenched and only Lady Francis' glare stopped him from going after the man again. "In other words you're saying I'm lying!"

"T'is not lying I'm thinking. There's nae doubt, nae doubt at all that you and this gentleman," he bowed towards me, "found what you found. Nae doubt the creatures you described were as you described. I myself have set hand to that young pterodactyl you brought back, when I was but a wee lad. T'was quite real and quite, quite, lovely."

I nearly choked. The pterodactyl chick we'd brought back from South America, over ten years prior, could hardly be called lovely. But as far as I could tell, this young man felt differently. I kept my silence, more than a little taken aback. I did find a moment to wonder how he'd gotten his hands on the monster. It'd escaped and was last seen flying south-west for its homeland.

"If you don't think I'm lying and you don't think I'm mistaken and you admit to having met my pet then what the devil do you mean, casting doubt on my work?"

Waving gloved hands to brush away the accusation, the young man told Professor Challenger. "What it is I'm saying, then, is the Lost World ought to be investigated for something more than the obvious. I'm knowing you planned an expedition...."

"One I was unable to complete, thanks to the fools of the scientific community. Including that instructor of yours." Professor Challenger remained bitter on the subject, as he'd looked forward to revisiting the Lost World and investigating its nature more thoroughly. Between the difficulties in finding suitable compatriots and the war, we'd had to put it off for some time now.

"Oh, aye. My Professor's a hard man t'work with, t'is true." The young man smiled in a genial way as he continued, "And t'is regrettable you weren't able to return. T'is the why of what you found that interests me. How could such things survive so long unchanged, when every other life on this world evolves over time? One species I'll grant. There've been other cases. But as many as you found? T'is mair to this than just chance."

Quite suddenly Professor Challenger's attitude changed. He slapped his hand against the strange young man's shoulder, a friendly blow that'd knocked bigger men than this one over. Yet again the man shifted, so most of the force struck thin air.

Ignoring the evasion, Professor Challenger waved a hand towards the hotel's little restaurant, where some of the unnerved hotel employees were hiding. "McKenzie's impossible to talk to," he said genially. "I'd expected more of the same from his student. Let's have a drink and discuss this further, Mr. ah... I didn't get your name."

"T'is your pardon I ask, Professor. The question of the Lost World was so interesting I was forgetting to introduce myself. I am Song Wulong." The young man bowed, while Lady Francis and I exchanged startled looks. Song Wulong was the name of the translator we were expecting to meet here, before we headed further east to Aksu.

Captain Wright sat up straight, his good humor gone in an instant. "You're that Chinee they hired for us? Take off your hat before a lady, boy. Don't you heathens have any manners?"

The young man's smile was startlingly sweet as he obeyed, revealing collar length straight white hair. Without bothering to acknowledge the good Captain, he murmured, "Aye, I'm being a rude beggar, not speaking up proper yet. I've been traveling the Tibetan Plateau for some time. Foxes and other wildlife are having nae use for European manners. Or Chinese, for that matter."

I stared at the young man, forgetting my own manners, startled as I was by his appearance. He was around medium height, slightly built, and startlingly attractive for a man. Without his cap to obscure his face it was easier to tell he was of Chinese descent, with soft features and slender eyes of some pale color.

He was also an albino.

Before I continue, dear reader, I should explain just how it was Professor Challenger and I, Edward Malone, found ourselves so very far from our native England.

This was not the first, nor—I hope—will it be the last time we travel to parts unknown, seeking esoteric knowledge and discoveries. This was, however, the first time we'd done so on the behest of the British Government. Accompanied by the aforementioned Lady Francis and Captain Wright, we'd spent months in trains, carriages and various other vehicles, crossing Europe and Western Asia.

Seeing as how we were on a mission involving National Security, this document is not intended for the general public. Nonetheless, I shall treat it as I would a report for my paper, as I would find it difficult, nay, impossible, to write in a more official manner.

Our purpose in leaving our beloved island came about soon after Professor Challenger and I encountered Theodore Nemor. As I have written elsewhere, Nemor had invented a device capable of transforming solid matter to some peculiar plasma and back again. It was a device he intended to sell to the highest bidder. Indeed, he'd implied he'd already done so and was only waiting to be paid before handing it and its plans to its new owner.

Nemor may have been a brilliant scientist but he lacked common sense. He was foolish enough to place himself in the way of his machine during his demonstration. When Professor Challenger—accidentally, I'm sure—started it, Nemor was hoist on his own petard.

Soon afterward, Professor Challenger notified the proper authorities on the matter, not wanting the machine to fall into the wrong hands. This, in turn, led to him being contacted by an unnamed government agency. One who—by means I am not permitted to repeat—persuaded Professor Challenger to study Nemor's machine and the origin of the crystal that appears to power it.

Professor Challenger brought me into the case, citing my knowledge of world affairs and investigative journalism. And I, in turn, determined that Nemor apparently hailed from a region of Asia known as Kyrgyzstan, specifically the aforementioned city of Aksu. At least that was the furthest I was able to trace him without actually following his path.

Towards that end, we were requested to travel to Aksu and seek Nemor's origin. Our purpose was in part to discover how his disintegration ray actually worked. As one might expect, the source of the strange crystal powering his device was also considered important. Apparently it possessed hitherto unknown properties that left the government scientists who'd studied it mystified.

I didn't know if we could find more of those crystals or how we'd get them back if we did, but that was the job of our companions, not myself or Professor Challenger.

Up to the point where I began my report, our party consisted of myself, Edward Malone, reporter for the Daily Gazette; Professor George Edward Challenger, the famed scientist whose discoveries and personality so often shocks the scientific community; Lady Francis Dennistoun, daughter of the Viscount of Midsomer Marsh; and Captain Jeremiah Wright, late of His Majesty's Army and another member of that aforementioned government agency.

Readers will know Lady Francis' many exploits from the papers; her meeting with the Dalai Lama; her time spent as a *gaucho* in South America; and, of course, her escape from Bolsheviks in Siberia. During the Great War, she spent a number of months behind enemy lines, assisting British Nationals in their escape from harm's way.

She was a small gingery woman of slightly over middle age. Tough and muscular, she'd a no nonsense way about her that tended to overcome most obstacles. Professor Challenger was, of course, a man of a different caliber than most, so the two of them often locked heads when it came to what their plans should be. If she, or rather the British Government, weren't in charge of our coffers I believe they'd have fought a great deal more often and a great deal longer.

Captain Wright was nearly Lady Francis' exact opposite. Tall where she was short, skinny where she was heavier-set, young where she was older. His black hair was cut ruthlessly short and his dark grey eyes were sharply intelligent. He'd an odd way of muttering to himself, one I suspected was partly driven by the Professor's personality. If he weren't under orders to cooperate I'm sure blows would've been exchanged a long time earlier.

I have described both myself and Professor Challenger elsewhere. Let it be said I remain plain, decently tall and clean-shaven. Professor Challenger is as broad and muscular as ever and there are but few grey hairs in his thick black curls.

Our last companion was to be a Chinese national, the son of a diplomatic liaison, educated in Great Britain and hired to assist us in our travels. Up until now we'd been able to find enough people who could understand at least one of the five or six civilized tongues Lady Francis and I spoke, but that'd change once we reached Aksu. There weren't many Europeans that far into the hinterlands.

That Song Wulong was an albino was unexpected but explained why I'd initially thought him a European. Indeed, even now it was hard to tell, for his glasses mostly hid the characteristic tilt to his eyes. Their color was uncommon to his race, but I knew just enough about albinos to expect they'd be bright red or some other light shade.

According to Lady Francis, Song Wulong was from a place called Sichuan, the oldest son of some local lordling. He'd been sent to Great Britain to study and I'd assumed he'd done so at Oxford, Cambridge or the College of London. Now I understood I was wrong. His speech was pure Edinburgh.

In the end, of course, it hardly mattered. As long as Song was capable and tough enough for our coming journey I'd little doubt he could handle the small disasters such groups are often heir to. Our employers surely wouldn't add a fragile doll to our passenger list. Especially since Professor Challenger's penchant for drawing attention and trouble remained as strong as it was the day we'd first met.

As I recall, he'd tried to throttle me as well.

With our last party member arrived it wasn't long before we were once more on the road. Up until now, we'd been able to find hotels along the way. There were enough small towns and cities to allow us comfortable beds. Once we set off for Aksu, however, our sleeping arrangements became more difficult.

Indeed, everything between Kashgar and Aksu was a great deal rougher than it had been. The road was frequently traveled, yes, but the terrain it passed through was rocky and mountainous. When it rained, which was fortunately seldom, the road became impossible to pass, forcing us to wait for it to dry again. Dust storms rose up in turn, once again bringing us to a halt.

Our road from Kashgar to Aksu was just a bit under 500 kilometers. If we'd a better cart and the weather cooperated we could have made the trip in a fortnight. With neither available, the best we could do was just about twenty kilometers a day.

I spent my days sketching amusing moments from our trip. Captain Wright lounging in the shade, resembling nothing so much as a sleepy lizard. Professor Challenger shedding layers of clothing until all he had was a light cotton shirt, native trousers and a broad rimmed straw hat. Lady Francis, elegant in a tan split skirt and jacket, perching on the driver's seat beside Song. Song himself caring for the horses and having his hair nibbled on as he gave them their water.

By the time we'd reached Kashgar we'd long since worn out most topics for conversation except for the sights surrounding us. Song at least gave Professor Challenger a new audience.

"Why do you care what he thinks about partogansees or whatever it is at home?" Captain Wright demanded at one point. "You're our translator, Chinee. You just do your job—when we have a job for you to do—and keep out of your betters' business."

To be fair, it'd been a perfectly miserable few days. Those storms I mentioned earlier had forced us to a halt and we were now sweltering in the sun as we waited for the road to dry. Between that and Song's ability to seem perfectly at home and comfortable no matter what the circumstances Captain Wright was in a terrible mood.

Song bowed politely and spoke in an oddly formal way. "This lowly son of his father is little import, t'is true. But this student's field of study is biology. Specifically, this one studies reproduction. E'en more specifically, he studies parthenogenesis."

I must have shown my confusion. The term was one I'd not run across in my travels with Professor Challenger. My friend grinned at me, teeth white amid his sweat damped whiskers. "Parthenogenesis is when a female of a species gives birth without access to a male. The offspring is invariably female as well..."

Captain Wright snorted for some reason and Song coughed. "T'is sorry I am for contradicting you, Professor, and I'll ask you not to break my skull afore I finish...."

A glare. A sigh. They had some variation of this conversation frequently and only rarely did Professor Challenger ever manage to lay hands on our translator. The one time he did he released Song quickly, after the young man poked him in the elbow. He never did explain why.

"Well? What nonsense are you going to spout this time?"

"T'is only that I've seen the female offspring rule t'is nae always the rule. My family's zoo had a lizard named Nulong and the sweet wench kept gifting us with boys." His expression turned sad as he added, "They're gone, unfortunately. Them and all my family's lands."

I latched onto the only thing I actually understood from the discussion. "*Long* as in dragon, right? Like your name?"

That set Song chuckling. "Nae, Mr. Malone, though I can see where you'd think that. The *long* in my name means rising moon. Appropriate to one of my coloring, aye?"

Aggravated, for reasons I still could not quite lay finger to, Captain Wright grumbled, "Who the hell cares what a heathen Chinee calls himself?" Something made him turn away, muttering to himself again, and I'd swear he was annoyed with himself for his rudeness.

In any other place and time, Captain Wright's unpleasant manners might have resulted in a spat. Instead, Song turned back to Professor Challenger. "I did nae get your thoughts on the matter we were discussing though. And t'is aware I am that my family's pet might be some odd sort of outlier. But do ye think it possible the mechanism for parthenogenesis varies from species to species?"

The rest of the afternoon was spent on a discussion that could have been in Greek for all the sense it made to me.

As we traveled to Aksu I couldn't help noticing just how odd Captain Wright's behavior was. That he was horribly rude to all of us, especially Song, could hardly be ignored. Indeed, there were moments when I was sure he wished to strike Song, only to back off and turn away before he could act on his anger.

It became so obvious that I finally found a private moment to ask Lady

Francis about the Captain. "He seems troubled. Mumbling to himself. Tripping over his own feet as if he wants to go two directions at once. And his treatment of Song is nothing short of insolent."

"He's always been short-tempered," Lady Francis admitted. "But he seems to have gotten worse since his accident."

I'd heard nothing of an accident until now and when I raised a brow, she explained, "It was he who was put in charge of the disintegration ray. In the process of moving it to our laboratories for investigation, he was struck down. A live wire where he didn't expect one, from what I understand. Had him speaking in tongues for days afterwards. The poor man barely knew which foot to use when."

"Surely it would have been better to let him recover, rather than sending him on this investigation, though?"

Lady Francis looked amused, spreading her hands helplessly. "That was over six months ago. He's quite well, aside from his oddly short temper. It would have been an insult to remove him from the case simply because of a minor electric shock. He's been through far worse over the years."

I supposed she was right. The Captain was a dedicated member of our Government. Moreover, I was sure the agency to which he and Lady Francis owed their loyalty would have made certain he was well enough to fulfill his role. "I suppose I'm mostly worried he'll offend our translator and send him packing."

"Mr. Song is a diplomat's son, Mr. Malone. I think we can rest assured that he will not casually abandon us." She glanced our pale-haired companion's way, adding, "Besides, if he can take your Professor Challenger's insults without ever losing that smile of his, I sincerely doubt Captain Wright will be able to drive him away."

Considering Challenger was that very moment threatening to throw Song in a scorpion pit, I was very much afraid she was right.

Our travels were, for the most part, unremarkable. One incident, however, did make us all quite glad of Captain Wright's presence. I've no doubt we would have been captured, possibly dragged off as slaves, if not for his quick thinking.

We'd settled in for the night in a single large tent at the side of the road. Lest anyone take concern that we were three men sharing space with an unmarried

A live wire where he didn't expect one...

lady, I hasten to note the tent was divided in such a way as to prevent our seeing anything of our companion that we should not. As for the four of us remaining, only two ever slept at one time, so we'd little trouble fitting inside.

I'd long since learned it was impossible to sleep near Professor Challenger without some sort of earplugs. The set I brought with me were quite solid, almost enough to keep the Professor's snores from disturbing me. They were also more than enough to conceal any night noises from outside our tent.

This was, of course, not entirely a good thing, for it forced Captain Wright to be quite rough waking me from my sleep, a good hour after I'd lain down. He set a hand to my lips before I could react. "I'd wake Challenger first," he whispered urgently in my ear. "But that'd alert the enemy."

Given how loudly Professor Challenger was snoring right then, I understood his point. Except, "Enemy?"

"A half dozen armed men are creeping around the camp," Captain Wright told me. "The Chinee is keeping watch, in case they get too close. I figure they're waiting for the moon to set."

The moon was just a bit past half-full and I'd noted how beautiful its light was, shining on the sands of the desert to our south. Once it set, our only light would come from the stars and the banked fire just outside our tent. Not nearly enough to see by, if someone chose to approach.

I inclined my head, sliding my hand around my rifle and carefully crawling out of the tent to join Song. Captain Wright shifted around behind me, just barely audible beneath the noise of Professor Challenger's snores. A moment or so later Lady Francis said, quite loudly and complainingly, "For God's sake, Professor. Would you please stop that confounded snoring?"

Professor Challenger snorted. Almost sounded like he was waking up. A moment later he was snoring again, albeit softer. I knew from long experience that he would not, could not, have done anything of the sort if he were truly asleep. At a guess Captain Wright had told him to continue making noise once he'd been roused enough to be warned.

I found Song mounted on one of our horses, acting like a parent soothing a child. "T'is just a wee night beast crawling round, little 'un. Nae reason t'fash yerself."

The beast was nervous, too. It kept shifting around, so I was sure Song would be thrown any moment. His balance was excellent, however, and he remained where he was without trouble. I waited, examining the landscape, trying to spot the enemy.

Our campsite was nestled in a crack in the hill along the north side of the roadway. Judging from the blackened rocks above us, it'd been used since time immemorial, a favorite safe place for travelers in this remote and desolate place. Captain Wright hadn't liked it, but the only other choice would have left us vulnerable on all sides from attack.

It took several minutes squinting before I spotted huddled figures amid the rocks above, a sight that sent a thrill of bitter memory through me. The beast-men of the Lost World had approached us so, their clever fingers and toes giving them purchase where no human could have found it.

Surely there were no such creatures here. These lands were desolate, yes, but they were traveled. No beast or foul monster could possibly hide here unknown to modern man. No, our enemies were almost certainly human. At least I hoped they were.

Pretending to stretch, as if it were time for my watch, I sauntered to the fire, scanning the rocks casually. Now I knew where the enemy lay, I could overlook them as if they were not there. Years of traveling with Professor Challenger had taught me the way of it.

"The horses all right, Song?" I asked, coming over to our translator.

"Oh, aye. Just a bit hot and bothered. There's a little wildcat wandering out there and I'm thinking they caught its scent."

By now I knew Song's habit of regarding even the biggest and most unpleasant of beasts as small and sweet. He might've been lying for the sake of our would-be attackers, though I doubted it. The enemy most likely didn't speak English and wouldn't know what he was saying. Likely there was a wildcat out there and I doubted it was as friendly as he pretended.

"Well, I do hope it stays away from us."

"Aye. Would hate to be having to harm it just for the sake of our skins."

The light from the moon faded as it sank further into the western sky. As it did, I watched the enemy gather themselves. Seeing Captain Wright slipping out of the tent, moving slow and steady, I prepared myself. It wouldn't be long.

The first attacker was impetuous. He leaped towards the tent itself, dagger glinting in the darkness, aimed for the center. Another leapt in from the other side of the crack, also aiming for the tent. No doubt it was Professor Challenger's noise attracting them.

Two rifles fired at once; mine and Captain Wright's. His was the more accurate. His target landed in the dirt and lay still. Mine, on the other hand, screamed and struggled to get upright. I fired again, angry at myself for having aimed poorly.

A third and fourth man leapt for the horses, and the one Song rode reared up, hooves flailing. Its companion followed suit, its whinny a scream of rage and terror. Those hooves smashed into the men's skulls, killing them instantly.

Captain Wright fired again, this time at the sneakier of our attackers. This one had been slowly and carefully lowering himself into the crack and sliding towards the tent. Once again his shot took our enemy down before he'd a chance to react. At the same time Professor Challenger flung himself out of the tent.

With a shout, he grabbed one more of our attackers, throttling him without hesitation. At the same time, Lady Francis appeared at the tent flap, her little pistol's shot a soft yip among the louder barks of our rifles. It was still just as effective. The man in Challenger's grasp went limp.

As the night fell silent again, Captain Wright said, "And now you see why I didn't like this spot for a campsite."

It still being night we had no choice but to drag our would-be attackers' bodies away from our campsite and try to get a bit more sleep. From the sound of things, the wildcat Song mentioned found the remains and set to disposing of them. I didn't look forward to seeing the results of the meal the next morning.

To my surprise, there wasn't much left of our attackers. Blood, yes, thick and dark and spread all over the sand, attracting flies. A few torn pieces of flesh. A couple of bones, gnawed almost beyond recognition.

"How many of those beasts were there?" I demanded, staring at the results in confusion. "Surely one cat could not have eaten so much. Even our attackers' clothes are gone."

Professor Challenger set a hand on my shoulder, the light squeeze clearly intended to calm my fears. "There's no sign, of course, but I think the bodies were taken away deliberately."

Did he mean our attackers had allies who'd chosen to remove the bodies rather than attack us again? If so, why would they do such a thing? I doubted it was piety or consideration for their cohorts' remains. They'd left too many torn pieces behind for that to be the case.

Off to the side, Captain Wright made an odd grumbling noise. But when we looked at him, he waved off our curiosity. "Something must have dragged them off. Let's not borrow trouble. It's got nothing to do with us."

"One odd thing," the good Professor offered. "This femur." He held up the bloodied thing as if he meant to hand it around. If so, only Song took him up on the offer, accepting the remains without turning a hair. "It's deformed."

"Aye, and it is." Song turned the thing around and examined it carefully, looking a bit like he were handling a turkey leg and not a human being's. "Th' third trochanter t'is mair developed than I'd be expecting. And t'is a wee bit on the short side."

"That could just be because it was broken off," Professor Challenger offered, though I could tell he was poking holes in Song's observations to test him.

"Aye, but look, th' shape of th' broken end suggests it was close to th' joint. See, t'is enlarging...."

Captain Wright growled a curse, grabbing the femur and tossing it far out into the sands to our south. "Leave the damned thing be. I don't care what happened to those bodies. I just want to get to Aksu before we have more bandits on our heads!"

He was right, of course, though I could tell from both Professor Challenger and Song's expressions that they'd like to investigate the matter further. Still, they didn't argue. Just climbed back onto the cart so we could continue on our way.

As we rode, I couldn't help looking back the way we'd come and wondering. One doesn't become a newspaper reporter on the strength of one's grammar and writing alone. The longer one was at the job, the better one's intuition became, and mine was screaming at me to pay attention.

Somehow, I was sure we hadn't heard the end of last night's battle. Not in the slightest.

It would be incorrect to say the rest of our trip to Aksu went smoothly but we had no more attacks in the night. The road remained difficult to navigate, however. We were all, even the ever cheerful Song, deeply grateful when the first signs of greenery came into sight. Aksu's farms appeared soon after, stretching around the central city, an emerald gleaming amid dusty gold, bounded by dark blue canals.

It wasn't long after we arrived at the edge of the oasis that we met our first locals. Farmers, busily working their fields, mostly too busy to pay attention to strangers. Captain Wright gestured at Song. "This is your job. Go find out where Hafiz Ihsan lives."

Hafiz Ihsan was the owner of the farm Theodore Nemor had leased while he resided in Aksu. From our correspondence I knew the land had belonged to his wife's parents and wasn't fertile enough to make much of a living off of. With Nemor gone and his lease long since over, Hafiz Ihsan was glad to let us take a look at what was left behind. For, naturally, a price.

Song did his job quickly and efficiently. Within an hour Hafiz Ihsan's son, Mahir, was guiding us to the farm. Mahir was a skinny teen with dark brown hair and skin and amazingly intense green eyes. He even spoke a bit of English, thanks to his father having studied at the University of London. He was not proficient however and was happy to let Song do most of the translating.

Song and Mahir hit it off right away, much to Captain Wright's irritation. It was obvious he didn't trust either our guide or our translator. Equally obvious he hated not being able to understand what they were saying. And obvious, too, he suspected the pair were laughing at him every time one or the other chuckled.

After a little while Song told us, "Mahir is sayin' there's a tale his grandparents' place is haunted. His father t'is not believing it, of course, being a God-serving Muslim and nae believer in superstition."

While Captain Wright sniffed, Professor Challenger grumbled. "Hauntings? Nonsense indeed. No such thing as ghosts."

"T'is what they believe, not I." Song grinned cheerfully. "T'is only recent they seem to have done so. Mahir claims the ghosts were nae around when his grandparents lived there."

I wondered aloud if Nemor had left a device to protect his property from spies. "Though I suppose Hafiz Ihsan would have noticed if that were the case. He's surely been there since Nemor's rent lapsed."

By this time we drew close to the southern edge of Aksu's farms. None terribly large and all carefully irrigated, they were mostly cotton fields, with a few wheat and barley in between. For the most part the farms were in good condition, with water from Aksu river feeding into their irrigation channels.

The further from the river we got, however, the dryer and less fertile the farms grew. They were smaller, too, with fewer workers tending the fields. I could see why Hafiz Ihsan didn't bother farming the land. Eking out a living here would be nearly impossible.

Mahir pointed at a few dilapidated buildings at the center of a weed covered field. Surprisingly, the irrigation channel surrounding the land was filled with water and the plants along the edge were bright green against the dusty brown and yellow surrounding it. I'd have expected the channels to be let to dry, given nothing grew in the field they surrounded.

The house wasn't terribly large. More a hut just big enough for a small family. There was a stable towards the back and I could see farming implements hanging on its inside walls as we passed its open door. The place felt sad. Uncomfortable. "I can see why someone might think it's haunted," I muttered.

"Nonsense," Captain Wright snapped, jumping off the cart so he could go to the hut's door and check inside. It took him but a few minutes to return.

"Nothing useful in there." He turned to Song. "Ask the boy if there's a cellar."

Song obeyed and a moment later answered, "He's saying there is, but t'is all blocked up. There were an earthquake, it's seeming. Just a bit after Nemor was leaving, in fact."

"I find it hard to call that a coincidence," Professor Challenger muttered.

"Oh, and you think Nemor has the power to cause earthquakes along with his ability to disintegrate what he feels like?" Wright demanded, though his worried expression suggested he feared that very thing.

"If he has... had... the ability to disintegrate anything, he likely had other tools at his command," Professor Challenger snapped in turn. "It hardly matters. We'll have to find a way into that cellar. Nemor's work is most likely there."

We set up camp in the old hut, leaving young Mahir to do the cooking for us while we looked for a way into the cellar. As Mahir had said, the stairwell leading down was full of debris. Nothing large, but it'd take some time to make our way through.

"We could hire some men to assist us," Lady Francis murmured, gazing at the mess with a dismayed expression.

"Need I remind you our employers want to keep outsiders out of this as much as possible? We already have too many." Captain Wright looked thoughtfully at Professor Challenger. "There's not enough room in that stairwell for more than one man at a time, anyway. Malone and I are strong enough to handle the smaller items. Professor Challenger can surely manage the larger. Unless, of course, he's too good for manual labor?"

Professor Challenger sniffed. "Of course I'm not too good for manual labor. I didn't get this build sitting around the house reading and making notes."

"T'is anything ye'd have me do?" Song asked suddenly. "I cannae speak for Lady Francis o'course, but I promise, I'm nae as weak as yer thinking I look."

Lady Francis added, "At the very least, the two of us can organize what you bring out. Most will be debris from the stairwell, of course, but it's possible the further you get in, the more of Nemor's things you'll find."

Though I could tell Captain Wright wasn't terribly pleased by the offer, he finally admitted Lady Francis was right. "We'll use the stable to store things, then. And don't expect much from this. An earthquake doesn't play favorites. It won't be just the stairwell damaged, but everything down there."

"Not everything," Professor Challenger corrected. "The ground above would have fallen in. I see no sign whatsoever of such a thing."

He was right, too. The farmyard was paved with clay bricks, weeds growing out from between them. Those bricks were a trifle uneven but not a single one looked like the foundation beneath had settled or moved so much as an inch in the last century.

"Indeed," Song added. "T'is another question for ye. If th' stairwell were blocked by earthquake, would nae the whole place show th' signs, as badly damaged at that stairwell is? The house might stand and stay standing, but I'm finding it hard t'believe th' stable's untouched."

Captain Wright sneered, obviously displeased at the contradictions. "We'll see, then. Let's just get to work and find out."

Between the Captain and I, we cleared half the debris in that stairwell out and into the stable that afternoon. Professor Challenger, as promised, used his remarkable strength to drag the heavier pieces out. He even stabilized the passage, holding the supports steady while Captain Wright and I replaced the broken struts.

We found nothing worth commenting on; Broken stones from the stairwell walls; Broken struts from the supports. A few dozen scorpions made things more interesting but typical of the man, Song happily removed them from danger.

By evening we were inside the laboratory and faced with a horrible mess. The ceiling might not have fallen in, but the earthquake had tossed everything around so badly it'd take hours, possibly days, to make sense of everything. In the end, we decided to wait until the next day to begin sorting through the ruins.

Mahir made an excellent dinner for us, a spicy stew of chicken meat and vegetables I'm afraid I didn't recognize. Flat breads accompanied the meal, as well as some bright red peppers that Song warned him to leave out. Apparently they were quite hot, a fact I learned to my sorrow after trying one.

"T'is not unlike me homeland's cooking," Song told me while I choked on the raw red-hot taste. "Here. Eat th' bread. It'll help."

Professor Challenger grinned at me and I could tell he'd known what I was getting into when I'd taken a pepper. I made a note to ask about foods I didn't recognize and ruefully settled on just the stew.

When night fell we set up watch. I wasn't entirely sure we needed to do so, now we were in civilization and safely within solid walls. But Captain Wright was adamant and he was in charge of security.

My turn to sleep came soon enough and I slept heavily, dreaming strange dreams. Lifted from my bed like a child, surrounded by strange scents and even stranger voices. Movement down a set of steps. Cold grey mist and a dark dank passage. Musty smells that reminded me of the snake house at the London Zoo. Sounds, echoing into the distance.

Despite the strangeness I slept calmly, barely aware of being lain down upon cold stone, dimly hearing the sound of scraping metal. I felt comfortable, as if something reassured me that all would be well. As if it were telling me I was in no danger at all.

The dream lied. I woke with a start in darkness so complete I was sure I'd gone blind. Professor Challenger's hand was on my shoulder, his voice in my ear. "Stay calm. We've been kidnapped."

They were not sentences I felt should be spoken anywhere near each other. I certainly didn't want to obey. But I'd learned, over my years of working with the Professor, that he was always right on such subjects. It wouldn't do to panic. "The others?"

"T'is but Lady Francis and I," Song answered from somewhere near. "Nae sign of th' Captain, nor Mahir, neither. I'm hoping th' lad's in no danger. T'would be wrong if he were injured, when all he were doin' were helping us."

I couldn't disagree, but right that moment I was more interested in where we were and how we'd come to be there. Fortunately, before I had a chance to ask, Professor Challenger was already answering my question. "I can't speak to our location. I can say I believe we're some distance below the earth."

"Why do you think that?" Lady Francis asked, though neither she, nor I, argued. Some instinct suggested the Professor was quite right in his belief.

"By the type of stone surrounding us, the ambient temperature and the air pressure." I heard the Professor slap the wall, adding, "The stone is granite and quite dense. The temperature and air pressure is quite a bit higher than it would be closer to the surface."

"But how did we get here," I demanded. "We certainly didn't walk."

"As to that...."

"Yes?"

"I have no answer. I only know what my semi-aware mind took note of. A sensation of traveling downwards through a confused mist."

It was the same dream I'd had and now I was awake the calm I'd felt earlier was gone. "And where are we now?"

"Imprisoned, as best I can tell. I've a lighter, of course, and have made use of it to get an idea of our location. But I don't wish to waste the fuel and I'd

...we are some distance below the earth.

rather not set anything alight until I have to. The less attention we draw from our captors—and make no mistake, we are captive—the better."

I slumped where I sat, glumly aware that of the four of us, I was the one closest to panic. No matter how many times I found myself in such a situation I could never quite grow easy with it. "Do you have a plan?"

"Song has been listening for voices and thinks he hears some human language in the distance."

Song coughed. "I'd be lying t'say I were sure it were human, or at least homo-sapiens, Professor."

"What else could it be, though?" Lady Francis demanded.

"As to that, I cannae say. T'is only that I'm remembering the Professor's come across people not quite fully human afore."

We had indeed. The beast-men of the Lost World didn't have a language we could understand, but they'd communicated with each other well enough. And there'd been other instances, a trip to Borneo that'd led us to a forgotten tribe closer in kinship to orangutans than human. And Professor Challenger was convinced the people who'd lived in an ancient city in the far north had been off-shoots of another line of evolution, one that'd failed to thrive when their younger and faster cousins arrived.

"Whatever the language is, whatever the people are who speak it, can you understand?" Professor Challenger asked.

"I hear but a word or so I recognize. T'is similar to a Western Chinese language, but I'd hae t' study it careful to be sure of anything." Song shifted position. Added, "I wouldnae like to be staying where we are and waiting, if leaving's possible, though. I'm hoping ye have a thought on how t'be getting us out?"

"While you three were still unconscious, I studied our prison carefully. There's a gate of wrought iron. One I believe I can lift. But I cannot lift it high enough to get out myself."

By which he meant the three of us could, probably, slip out from under the gate. When I said so, the Professor told me, "There has to be a mechanism on the other side controlling it. There's a good chance it'd be guarded."

"Which means I'll have to fight my way to it." I inclined my head, though none but I could know it. "All right. I'm up for it."

"Mr. Malone, I hope you don't think we intend to let you go alone," Lady Francis said firmly. "I promise you, I'm a useful woman in a fight, and having watched Mr. Song evade the good Professor, I've no doubt he's got a few tricks up his sleeves."

A chuckle came from Song's direction. "Well, now, Lady Francis, I will nae claim to have quite so many as my old father, but I ken how t'fight well enough."

"Then as soon as you are ready, I suggest you go." Professor Challenger paused. Added, "But not until you're sure you're strong enough. There's no point in escaping if it's just to be caught and dragged back again."

That was the voice of long experience speaking and I agreed wholeheartedly. There was no point in repeating the incident aboard the Incredulous and our trip to Moheli Island. Indeed, the less said about that whole embarrassing affair, the better.

If we'd food and water we might have stayed where we were a while longer, just to be sure we had the strength to handle whatever was to come. Lacking both, it made no sense to remain in place too long. We were thirsty, tired, and I—at least—was quite hungry.

Thus, as soon as I was satisfied I could stand and walk around, I enjoined Professor Challenger to do his part. It took him several minutes of effort to do so, not just because the gate was quite heavy but because he dared not let it make a sound as he lifted it. Its mechanisms were rusty and thus noisy.

At last I slid under the gate, Lady Francis and Song not far behind me. Beyond was a narrow passage, barely wide enough for two thin men to walk abreast. I set myself at the front and asked Song to take the rear.

Sounding amused, Lady Francis murmured, "You need not protect me, Mr. Malone. Mr. Song is smaller and weaker than I."

"T'is true," Song admitted. "And if I may, I'm thinking my eyesight might be best suited to this place, it being so dim and all."

Admitting he was right, I let him shift position and went side by side with Lady Francis instead. That way Song could watch for what lay ahead while Lady Francis and I could keep our hands on either wall, in case of an opening.

"How much can you see?" I asked as we made our slow and cautious way through the passage.

"Not much, I'm fearing. There's light way far ahead of us, but what we seek won't be so far."

Lady Francis murmured, "It wouldn't make sense, no. The mechanism has to be somewhere near."

We continued several yards, moving slow and mostly quiet, hoping our captors wouldn't come looking for us any time soon. It was, of course, a vain hope. We'd barely gotten far when Song set hands to my and Lady Francis' wrists. "Someone's coming."

As soon as he said so, I saw the light ahead growing slightly brighter. The sound of someone or something walking drew my attention. "Back the way we came," I ordered. It was the only way we could go.

The light brightened a bit more, still too dim to see much by, but now I could see the shadowy outline of my companions. We kept moving back and back, passing the gate to our prison, until finally we'd no choice but to stop. There were other cells along the way, but like the one we'd been in, they were all shut tight. They were empty, too, leaving me wondering where Captain Wright and Mahir might be.

As if the thought were enough to summon the man, I realized the person approaching was Captain Wright himself. Mahir was beside him, carrying a small globe that just barely lit the scene ahead of us. As the pair approached the gate, Challenger slammed into it, forcing both backwards.

"I'll throttle you!" Challenger shouted, trying to grab Captain Wright by whatever was handy. He missed, his arm just inches too short. "Not surprised you had something to do with this, Wright! You've been strange this whole trip! Now I see why, you traitor!"

"Despite appearances, I am not Captain Wright. Nor am I a traitor."

"The hell you aren't!"

"I am not. I borrow this one for the purpose of communication. His voice. His language. His body." Captain Wright, or whomever he was, drew an odd device from his pocket. A grey metal stick with a heavy knob at the end. Electricity crackled around the tip and he poked it at Professor Challenger's outstretched hand, forcing my friend back.

"You rotten bastard! Come in here and fight me like a man!"

"No. You and your companions are our prisoners until you agree to help."

I realized our captor couldn't tell that the Professor was alone in the cell. Likely Professor Challenger's bulk hid how empty things were behind him. This was our chance, possibly our only one, and I nudged Song to the side, waiting for a moment when our captor was most distracted by my friend's threats.

That moment came quickly and I rushed forward, tackling Captain Wright to the ground. He flailed, struggling against my grasp. Had the real Captain been in charge of his body, I've no doubt he would have defeated me handily. He was, after all, a trained soldier. The one controlling him, however, was not nearly so skilled. I managed to overwhelm him.

A heavy blow struck my shoulder. Mahir, struggling to help Captain Wright. Was he under some other's control the same way the Captain was? Or was it something similar to the force that'd brought us—unresisting—down into this dark place?

Song caught the boy by the wrist. Twisted his arm. Knocked him off his feet with a swipe of his foot. At the same time, Lady Francis pulled a fine cord out of the hem of her sleeve and used it to tie Captain Wright's feet for me.

Within moments we'd turned the tables on our captors and gained a light source. It wasn't bright, but it let me see the walls of the passage and realize we'd walked straight past a crank that surely must control the gate. Its placement was odd, barely three feet above the floor, as if it was intended to be controlled by someone quite a bit shorter than most people.

The gate was smaller than I'd expected, too. We hadn't noticed because we'd had to crawl out from under it earlier, but it was only five foot high. Were the builders midgets, then? The *orang* we'd met in Borneo had been rather small. Perhaps these beings were, too?

I turned the crank, which—in retrospect—was an error. The mechanism was old, in poor repair and just as noisy as it'd been when Professor Challenger had forced the gate open for us earlier. The sound echoed through the passage, its thunder silenced only when the gate finally rose to its full height.

A second of so later the noise of dozens of feet echoed from the passage ahead.

What came out for us were more people. Some seemed perfectly human, but a good number had a strange look to them, one that put me in mind of Theodore Nemor. They held rifles with a business-like air, warning me that they wouldn't hesitate to use the things if we gave them reason.

"Surrender now, if you please," Captain Wright managed to say from beneath me. "You cannot escape."

"I'm sorry, Professor," I muttered. "I should have expected this."

"You did what you had to," Professor Challenger answered. "We should have known it'd draw attention."

Captain Wright's body twisted beneath me and his controller said, "Release me."

I knew I'd no choice but to obey. I stood; watching for a chance I knew was unlikely to come. At the same time, Professor Challenger pulled Captain Wright to his feet.

"You're obviously not our good Captain. Who are you and how are you controlling him?"

"I can't say my name."

I couldn't help asking, "It's that secret, then?"

"No. A human mouth can't say it. I am Prince here. That must be enough." The person made a gesture to the two men at the forefront of the crowd. Spoke in a language that sounded a bit like the local lingo.

The crowd obeyed the being calling himself Prince and turned. At the same time he gestured. "You have no choice. Come with me. No more fighting."

Perforce, we let ourselves be led through the passage to a larger one. Other passages led off to the sides and I thought I could see dim lights moving somewhere within. Then we stepped out into what seemed like a starlit field.

It took me a moment to realize we were still far underground. That the stars were strange glowing insects, fluttering around the roof in huge numbers.

"Now that's putting me in mind of a glow-worm I've seen in New Zealand," Song murmured, cheerful as ever. "T'is nae a creature that flies, though, so I'm doubting they're related."

"Not fireflies, either," Professor Challenger agreed. "Or they'd be blinking."

Quite suddenly and surprisingly, Captain Wright snapped, "Don't you think we're in enough trouble without the two of you going on like that?"

I turned, startled, and saw the Captain's expression go from his usual embittered one to the calmer one I had to associate with the Prince. "Captain?"

"He is here. Controlling him is, you can guess, difficult." The Prince led us down a stone path between strange damp farms that looked like they'd been left to rot for some years. Ahead lay a building, not particularly imposing, its walls carved from the living rock. "I've had to let him be in charge for most of this trip."

"Your Highness," Lady Francis said, "If controlling our Captain is difficult, can I ask why you bother? Not to mention why you've taken us captive?"

"You'll get your answers soon enough. Be patient, or at least try."

We entered the building and soon found ourselves in a chamber containing a familiar object. The disintegration ray, its engine humming softly where it sat in the middle of the room.

"What in the world?" Lady Francis stared at the thing, her expression grim. "How did this get here?"

"I had it shipped ahead of us," the Prince said. A moment later he sniffed, the Captain taking charge again. "Abused my authority to do it."

"But... why?"

The Prince went to the machine. Turned to face us, gazing directly at the Professor. "We need your help, Professor Challenger. The one you called Theodore Nemor was one of us. A traitor who stole our ancestors' device and meant to use it to his own profit."

Professor Challenger considered the statement. "That much I believe. He was, quite clearly, quite obviously, a greedy swine with no morals whatsoever. But if you expect me to make that diabolical machine work for you instead, given its purpose...."

"Its purpose is not what you think, Professor." Gesturing at the crystal hanging amid the machine's works, the Prince added, "It's a tool, a way for our people to survive the long dry. And right now, this crystal contains nearly all of our race."

It took us all several minute to truly take in the Prince's meaning. It was Professor Challenger who spoke first, eyeing the machine thoughtfully. "You mean to say there are human beings trapped inside that thing?"

"For varying definitions of human, yes. The device transformed us to energy and stored us within the crystal."

"And you have no idea how to get them out yourself?"

"Professor, I've no doubt you could run a train engine if you chose. But do you think your King could? Do you think any person off the street could?"

I had to admit he made sense and said so. "Except,"

"Except?"

"How dare we trust your word. Right now you're controlling Captain Wright's body...."

"Not that I've had much of a choice," Captain Wright interjected, to the Prince's obvious annoyance. "You've been riding me ever since I took charge of this equipment and I'm not at all happy about it."

The Prince sighed. "Captain, it is your own fault I've been riding you. You're the one who activated the device, after all. If you hadn't, my mind would still be trapped inside, unaware of Nemor's treachery and our danger."

"It was my job!"

Lady Francis glared at the Captain. "I seem to remember you were explicitly told not to fiddle with the device."

Interrupting before an argument could break out between the two, or rather three, Professor Challenger asked, "One thing? When I activated the device back in London, what became of Nemor?"

"If you activated it correctly, he is stored within the crystal. If not, he's been scattered across the city. Of the two, the latter would be fit punishment for his treachery."

"And why did you bring the device here, instead of having me attempt to decipher its workings back in London?"

A confused look crossed the Captain's face. In a puzzled way, the Prince said, "This is our home. Why would I inflict your upper world environment on my people?"

"You said Theodore Nemor was a traitor. So he was one of you? How did he get his hands on the device?"

The Prince sighed. "He was of family entrusted the task of keeping the machine." He gestured upwards. "The river that flows above us drains a portion of its water into a reservoir. To fill it takes years. Decades. Sometimes centuries. In the dry time, Nemor's clan was assigned the task of keeping the device and releasing the rest of us from the crystal when the wet time comes."

"Instead he stole the thing, hoping to sell it." Song tilted his head curiously. "What of th' men helping ye? Th' ones outside."

"Some are of Nemor's clan. Others humans hired to help keep our secret."

A thoughtful hum escaped Song's lips. "Th' ones looking a bit like they're not fitting their clothes are your folk, then?"

"Yes."

"Could you lot stop jawing and do something about getting the two of us detached? I'm damn tired of having practically no control over my body."

Professor Challenger smiled. "One last question. What becomes of us when we've done what you want?" He gestured off the way we'd come. "Your actions do not inspire trust, sir. You've kidnapped us, dragged us miles underground and left us in a dark prison cell for some hours."

That made the Prince flush, which in turn set Captain Wright grumbling. But to his credit, he bowed apologetically. "Your race and ours are long separated, Professor Challenger. And having been bound mind to mind with this man, I know how we're likely to be treated. I wish only to assure the safety of my people. If you will forgive us the liberties, and accept the task, I will gladly repay you and send you safely home."

"Repay? By giving us some idea how the device works?" Lady Francis asked suddenly.

"Do you think it's a good idea for any country to have a thing like this? Captain Wright's knowledge tells me it was to be used as a weapon, and a terrible one at that." The Prince patted the device thoughtfully. "We use it to save our lives, but Nemor's treachery proves that there are things some would turn to war, no matter how innocent its original purpose."

The Captain harrumphed and was ignored.

Professor Challenger had but one last objection. "You realize when I used the device on Nemor, I did so in near complete ignorance, mimicking his setting in hopes I could stop him? Working out how to restore your people is out of my area of knowledge."

The Prince bowed politely. "We have old scrolls belonging to Nemor's clan, teachings that will help you understand, or so I hope. And if Mr. Song's resume is to be believed, he has a good understanding of the sort of old script those scrolls were written in. I beg you. There are five hundred lives trapped within that crystal. I would see them safe and free."

After a moment Professor Challenger sighed. "What can I do but agree? If only to try and understand just what that confounded thing of yours is doing."

Mahir was terribly apologetic once we'd agreed to help the Prince. Through Song's translation he explained, "My family has helped the Gurvel for generations. When the Prince contacted us, we were to help get you to the cavern."

If I was angry, it was only in that I would have preferred being asked to being forced into this place. Yet to be fair, it was true the Gurvel, whatever they were, might have reason to distrust the humans of the upper world. And they were not human as we understand human, that much was obvious.

I remembered the feeling of distaste I'd felt towards Nemor. The sensation of looking at something not quite right. The shape of his body alone had been peculiar, hunched and twisted beneath his loose-fitting clothes. His face had been thick and heavy, with a glossy unpleasant cast.

Now, waiting for Professor Challenger and Song to do their work, I couldn't help examining our captors, watching them for some sign of what they actually were. And the more I looked, the more certain I became that they wore masks formed of some waxy substance. The odd blemishes I'd noticed on Nemor's face were absent, but I wondered if the material he'd used had become damaged somehow?

Noting Captain Wright, and thus the Prince, approaching, clearly headed out into the cavern, I took it on myself to call out, "Might I join you, your Highness?"

"He's a nosy newspaper reporter," Captain Wright reminded the Prince mockingly. "Sure you want to be letting him poke around?"

The Prince eyed me. "Mr. Malone has a reputation for honesty. And all I'm doing is inspecting our fields. Hardly much of a secret." He gestured for me to follow.

As we walked out of his palace, such as it was, the Prince noted, "You are still wondering how you were brought here?"

I admitted it. "The Professor believes we're deep below the surface. But for the life of me, I can't remember much of anything of how we were moved."

"The device Nemor would have sold as a weapon has many uses. A similar one is used to transport small groups a certain distance. I don't know how it

"Might I join you, Your Highness?"

works, so you needn't bother asking me."

Captain Wright harrumphed, "You just don't want to talk about it."

"That too, Captain."

It surprised me that the Prince was allowing Captain Wright to speak so readily. When I said so, he spread his hands. "His mind is quite strong, Mr. Malone. I was able to gain his support in this matter, but only because he hopes to be free of me once this is over."

"I damned well better be free of you when this is over, you bastard! The only reason I didn't ask for help was no one would've believed me."

When I thought about it, Captain Wright was likely correct. The Prince surely wouldn't have cooperated with him if he'd tried to ask for help. His only option was to have this person's mind and his bound for the rest of his life or to assist the Prince in his efforts.

It occurred to me that the Captain's superiors wouldn't be best pleased with him, given he'd essentially stolen a powerful device from their hands. One that could have become a useful weapon in the future. And, thinking of that, I had to admit I was glad he had. Somehow, I didn't think this was a Pandora's box we should open.

As we walked through the cavern I admit to gawking like a country boy in the city. It wasn't that everything was terribly impressive. Quite the contrary, in fact. There were no real houses, just holes in the wall of the cavern that might be like the caves we'd discovered back in the Lost World.

The land around us was marked off by stone paths going between field upon field of something similar to mushrooms. Whatever they were, they were small and numerous. They also had a faint, earthy, smell. "This is your people's food?"

"Yes. We have domesticated animals, but they're bound in the crystal with my people." The Prince eyed the fields with a satisfied air. "The fungus, however, needs nothing but for the ground to turn damp in order to grow."

I was about to ask more questions when I noticed a commotion towards one side of the cavern. There was an opening there, one that led into near total darkness. Only a few flickering lights showed a dim passage leading elsewhere. One from which shouts and shots echoed.

The Prince and I ran towards the opening, just as one of his people came running out. The man's mask was torn, revealing oddly tinted hide beneath. I didn't have time to look more closely, however, for the man gasped something that might have been language but sounded more like a bird chirping.

The Captain's face paled with the Prince's startled reaction. He spoke rapidly in that odd language from earlier and the man turned and ran back the way he'd come.

"What's wrong?" I demanded. "And please don't pretend there isn't anything."

The Prince was already headed for his palace. "Remember those bandits? They belong to the same group as Nemor. I'd hoped there weren't many left, but... it seems I'd hoped wrong." He gestured behind us as he ran. "There's a good fifty coming our way, intending to steal the device."

We found the others still hard at work; Lady Francis copying whatever Song read off word for word while Professor Challenger made notes on the wall. He ran his hands through his hair, ruffling it into a wild rats' nest as he examined the diagrams on the scrolls and compared them to the device.

"I've found the part scroll five mentions. It wasn't attached, so I'll have to work out where it fits. Those agents of yours could have done a better job dismantling this thing, you know."

"I'm sorry," Lady Francis began, sounding mildly disgruntled. Whatever she meant to say beyond that, however, she forgot when she saw the two of us enter and noticed Captain Wright, or rather the Prince's, expression. "What happened?"

"We're under attack. I'd hoped Nemor didn't have too many allies, but it's not looking good." The Prince glared back the way we'd come. "The rebels are surely armed. My people defend against them, but it's only a matter of time. I beg you, please finish your task quickly. Our only hope is for you to restore my people."

"T'is nae easy task ye set us, Yer Highness. I'm thinking it might be impossible."

That made Professor Challenger bristle angrily. "Are you saying I'm not up to it, you little...."

"Th' device is nae human technology, Professor. T'is lucky we are they borrowed th' languages of th' region when they wrote these scrolls. But are they enough?"

There were few things that put Professor Challenger into a fury, but having his ability questioned would always be one of them. Before he could grab the smaller man, Song added, "Of course, t'is apologies I'll be owing you, if you manage despite yourself."

That made Professor Challenger stop and grab the notes Lady Francis had put together. "Your Highness, what happens when the device activates correctly?"

"There are transport crystals set in all the walls of the cavern. My people will be restored in the positions they'd been when they were sent into hibernation."

The Professor made a satisfied noise. "All right. This is going to take a little while. I want all of you to get out and do something about keeping those rebels of yours from getting in. Meanwhile, I have an idea. If I can figure out how your machine works, I'll try it."

The Prince looked suspicious. "You have the look of one intent on doing something dangerous. I do hope you know what you're doing."

"Don't worry. If I'm right, it won't hurt at all. Run along, now, and let me work."

We left Professor Challenger scanning the notes and muttering under his breath. Only when I was sure no one else could hear did I ask Song, "Did you do that on purpose?"

"Th' good Professor was dawdling. I'm thinking he was hoping for a reason t'fail." Song grinned at me brightly. "Nae blame t'him. He kens as well as I that these folk are nae true humans. Twas caution, not cowardice, that were slowing him down."

I too had noticed how far from human the people of this place were. Nor did I pretend I liked the idea of loosing them on the world. They had that one device of Nemor's. What if they had other, even more powerful, weapons? Yet right that moment our only chance of getting back home was to defeat the rebels and free the Prince's people. And hope against hope we were doing the right thing.

It was fortunate that the Prince had brought our supplies with us when he'd transported us to his cavern. We had rifles and ample ammunition. We also had just enough time to get to the caves in the cavern wall, giving us places to hide where we could pick off our enemies from safety.

Song remained at the palace, staying with the dozen or so guards. "I've nae great fondness for guns," he told us. "T'is better if I find another way to be handling a fight."

"Don't expect me to cry for you if you get yourself killed," Captain Wright snapped.

"Wouldn't dream of it, Captain Wright. But I'm hoping someone will tell my old father if I fall that I did nae run." Song took up a stance at the doorway, waiting calmly as we hurried on.

The Prince led us up a narrow ramp leading to a ledge overlooking the cavern. "I hope this will be good enough," he said as we set our equipment down. "Prepare yourselves and the Captain and I will keep watch."

It took but a few minutes for Lady Francis and I to check and load our rifles. Only when we were done and ready, did the Captain leave watch to myself while he prepared his own weapon. "You'll have to let me handle this, you bastard," he told the Prince.

"I'm aware. Your rifles are interesting weapons but I lay no claim to understanding the aiming of them. My people don't have such things."

Captain Wright satisfied himself with a grudging sniff as he checked and loaded his rifle. "Pay attention then. You might learn something."

We all three lay flat on the ledge overlooking the cavern and I reflected that the Prince might have no understanding of distance weapons but he'd chosen our vantage point well. Possibly he'd learned such things from the Captain. Possibly he was wise enough to know where best to place us. Either way, we were perfectly positioned for both protection and attack.

It wasn't long. The shouts from the cave below us grew louder and louder. Metal clanged against metal and stone. Someone screamed a high-pitched noise that didn't sound like any human cry. As the first dozen or so figures ran out of the cave, I saw why.

Thus far the men assisting the Prince had seemed like particularly ugly humans. Having been caught in a fight and had their masks torn from their faces, it was quite obvious they were nothing of the sort. Still unattractive, at least to my eyes, they had long muzzles, huge red eyes and not a single hair on their heads. Their skin was pale and leathery, almost scaled in places. Some had lost their shirts in the fight, revealing slender, snake-like bodies covered in a strange, hexagonal, pattern.

"The hell," Captain Wright gasped. "That's what you lot look like?"

"And your reaction is why I will not inflict your people on mine," the Prince snapped back. "Look at how you treat your own allies, much less what you think aren't human."

Lady Francis sighed. Sighted down her rifle. "The enemy are the same as your allies, Prince. How do we tell them apart?"

"I ordered my people to retreat to the palace. Anyone attacking them will be enemies."

It made sense and it soon became easy to tell them apart by another means. The Prince's allies were dressed in clothing similar to that worn by the local villagers, but their attackers wore looser clothes more suited to the desert. The bandits who'd attacked us the other night had been similarly dressed, confirming the Prince's claim that these men were from the same group.

Most of the bandits belonged to the same race as their victims. Others were clearly human. They all cut down the Prince's allies without hesitation, firing their pistols into the others' backs. Some escaped. Some paused to help their fellows, only to be shot themselves.

I growled a curse and fired, unable to wait another moment. Lady Francis was but a second behind me and the Captain a moment or so later. As expected, our shots drew attention. But we had the high ground and better cover. They fired, but failed to harm us.

Within minutes the Prince's people had escaped into the palace. Song appeared among them, helping drag the injured in and occasionally cracking a few bandit skulls when they got too close. At the same time we shot to give him cover, forcing the enemy back.

With the bandits forced back, the Prince's people safe in the palace and ourselves keeping guard, we soon found ourselves at an impasse. The enemy couldn't reach us but we couldn't reach them. Sooner or later we'd run out of bullets and be just as helpless as those in the palace. From the bandits' manner, they knew we were trapped.

"We can't sit here," the Prince said, seeing our trouble. "There's a way to reach the other side of the cavern quickly, if you're willing to trust it."

I remembered what he'd said about how we'd been brought to this place. "That transportation device you mentioned?"

"Indeed."

"I don't like it," the Captain grumbled. "It's not canny."

I didn't like it either. I was about to say as much when I noticed something odd about the enemy. "Is it just me or are there fewer than there were before?"

Lady Francis swore in a most unladylike way. "Could they use that device of yours too?" she demanded.

Realizing her meaning and the danger, the only thing we could do was find cover and wait for the enemy to come at us yet again.

Our fears were soon proven right. We'd hidden in a nearby cave, using carved stone furniture for cover, peering through darkness into the dimly lit cavern. Within a few minutes some burly figures stepped quietly and cautiously into the cave.

One spoke, first in that chittering noise I'd heard earlier, then in one of the local languages. Neither were comprehensible but I didn't need to understand to guess their meaning. Surrender was demanded. I hesitated. Trusting these people didn't seem the best plan. Yet we didn't have an escape, either.

I was sure our fates were sealed when Song shouted loudly from somewhere outside, "Th'professor says, hold tight and pray!"

Guessing my friend was ready with his plan, I obeyed, grasping hold of the nearest object and closing my eyes. A moment later I felt an odd and familiar sensation. One I remembered only too well from the day we'd met Theodore Nemor and been introduced to his disintegration device. The world seemed to flicker, leaving me startled and disoriented. I stared around at my companions, only to realize I was alone.

I held my position, unsure of what to do, listening as someone came up to the entrance of the cave. To my relief, the Professor's voice spoke from outside. "I know you're in there, Malone. It's safe to come out now."

Never had I been so glad to hear my friend's voice. I stumbled out to join him and he grinned expansively and triumphantly at me, hands on his hips in a satisfied posture. "Well, now, I was beginning to worry that I'd never get you back. You were the last one I transduced, so it makes sense for you to be the last one reconstituted.

I stared at him. "Transduced? Reconstituted? I don't understand."

"I worked out that damned device and used it to turn everyone outside the palace to etheric energy. Then I restored everyone one by one. Mind you, it's a good thing I didn't touch the lot inside the palace or I'd have had one deuce of a time explaining things to these people." He gestured downwards at the cavern floor, where the Prince's people were setting their fungus farms to rights.

"But what are they?" I demanded. "Aliens, such as H.G. Wells suggested?"

Professor Challenger guided me down the ramp and towards the palace. "The Prince claims not. Says his people have been around longer than human. Song thinks they're descended from a species of dinosaur."

Dinosaur? "Is that even possible?"

"People didn't think the Lost World was possible until I proved it, Malone. And these folks' existence justifies Song's contention that we should investigate that place more carefully." The last the Professor said grudgingly, nor could I blame him. He didn't care for admitting ignorance.

By this time we'd reached the palace and I saw Captain Wright glaring down at some crates with a dour expression. Lady Francis sat nearby and if she didn't look entirely pleased, she didn't seem entirely unhappy either. "Ah, there you are, Mr. Malone. Now you've been restored, we can go back above ground."

"I still say we should make them give us more than just a few crystals and a scroll," Captain Wright grumbled. His voice and expression shifted as the Prince spoke through him again, adding, "Are you sure your people are remotely ready to understand the things as it is? Not to mention the political upheaval it'd create? You're better off with energy crystals."

I blinked at him. "You're still...."

"Thanks to whatever he did with our device, my mind is bound in his body," the Prince told me. "No one's sure how to undo it."

"And where would your people be if I hadn't?" the Captain demanded angrily.

"Still trapped and unaware and likely doomed. I didn't say I blamed you. But the result remains the same. We can't be free of each other."

"And that's something the two of you will have to work out for yourselves. The point remains, having accomplished our mission as best we can, it's high time we returned to home." Lady Francis sounded quite finished with everything and I couldn't blame her.

Noticing someone was absent, I asked, "Mr. Song?"

"Yer nae rid o'me that easy," Song said, coming in from a doorway. "You'll pardon me absence, I'm hoping. I was studying th' worms. Quite fascinating, how big they can get on th' right diet."

I had no idea what he meant and given some of the monsters we'd come across in our travels, wasn't at all sure I wanted to know.

Epilogue:

Our return home was uneventful. Captain Wright and the Prince came to a grudging agreement. The Captain had, after all, done what he'd been asked to. The Prince no longer controlled his body, though he occasionally did speak his mind when there were none but us to hear.

Lady Francis spent much of her time writing and rewriting her report. I've no doubt it was a complicated and infuriating process for her. She'd had a mission, after all, and though she'd come back with some useful items, she'd failed to bring home the main prize. But with so many of the people calling themselves the Gurvel there to stop her, she'd no choice but to accept what she could get.

Song and Professor Challenger went on as they began, arguing with increasing geniality over various subjects. Song, being focused entirely on his particular field of interest, could hardly keep up with the Professor when it came to matters like the operation of the Gurvels' device. Questions of biology and evolution, however, were subjects on which he could readily hold his own.

I don't think they ever quite agreed on the mechanism that had kept the Lost World locked so deep in the past. Song was convinced some external force was at work, whereas the Professor believed it was something to do with the area's ecology. Either way, they did agree further investigation was in order, and that they were the men to accomplish it.

It took some time before they actually managed to get the chance. Both were busy men and such an expedition was expensive. Needless to say when they did finally go, yours truly was their eager aide and documenter.

As to what they discovered? That, dear reader, is a tale for another time.

THE END

Challenging
Challenger

Professor Challenger wasn't my introduction to Sir Arthur Conan Doyle's work. Like many, I grew up on Sherlock Holmes. When I ran out of Holmes, I naturally sought out Doyle's other hero and found his most famous adventure, The Lost World. An adventure in the same vein as another favorite work—Journey to the Center of the Earth—I deeply enjoyed it and was sorry not to find more. (Drat the lack of the internet in my childhood days. So much research to be had.)

So when Ron decided to do an anthology of Challenger stories in the same vein as the Sherlock Holmes anthologies, I was definitely interested. With the internet on my side, I was able to get a copy of most of his later adventures and in the process found a short piece that gave me a beautiful foothold into Challenger's world; namely The Disintegration Machine.

Such a device couldn't possibly be left to unknown hands. Either those who'd intended to buy it or the British Government would have had to take a hand. And they, in turn, would have turned to the only man capable of working out the origin of the device and its creator, Theodore Nemor.

And thus, Challenger and his good friend and biographer set off to discover another lost world, meet strange beings and make new friends who may appear in other adventures later on.

After all, I do like a Challenge.

BARBARA DORAN - has been making up stories for as long as she can remember. From playing Ms. Marvel to her best friend's Captain Marvel to writing new stories for old characters (Hannibal King, X-Men, Green Hornet, The Saint, The Shadow and many others), to writing gaming and anime fanfiction online.

After ten years behind the keyboard as a software engineer, Barbara realized that her true love wasn't coding but making stuff up. So when she left that career in favor of dealing with two frequent interruptions of her life (namely her own personal Tiger and Dragon), she decided to use what little time they allowed her to work on writing. Her Long Suffering Husband, without whom she could never have managed such a goal, has been nothing if not supportive.

Along with reading every mystery, SF and fantasy book she could get her hands on, Barbara grew up watching Star Trek, Batman, Green Hornet, along with the usual Saturday morning cartoons. She became addicted to shows like Battle of the Planets and Doctor Who in her teens and discovered Run Run Shaw's martial arts flicks some years later. Those influences, along with a love of folklore and mythology, have become part of the world some small portion of her mind lives in. When, of course, she isn't chasing Tiger and Dragon from one school event to another.

Barbara can be contacted at <BarbaraDoran@sumergoscriptum.com>. Her website is <http://www.sumergoscriptum.com/barbaradoran/>.

What Rough Beast
by Michael Panush

Of all the various disasters, pestilences, social outcries, and crimes that I have covered during my career as a newspaper reporter, there are few that capture the interest of the public as much as war. Conventional wisdom long decreed that, for the purposes of selling papers, there was nothing as good as an honest conflict, preferably involving Tommy Atkins engaged in heroic combat with some nefarious foreigners.

The Great War, as it did with so many things, put an end to that.

In the year 1920, I found my readership entirely fed up with stories of conflict. And why wouldn't they be? We had but recently emerged from nearly half a decade of utter cataclysm, in which the casualty lists always had a place in the Times and so many of the sons of Suffolk and Lancashire met their ends on the Somme, or in the waters of Suvla Bay, or the sands of Arabia.

So stories pertaining to the new conflicts which arose, like aftershocks following a great quake, achieved little interest. The Russian Civil War, for instance, occupied a hazy section in the back of the great papers, and made only rare appearances in conversation pertaining to foreign affairs.

When the Russian Revolution first broke out, the sheer shock and novelty of the Bolsheviks rising up against the Tsar and the fiery birth of the Soviet Union had everyone talking—and fearful that the Red Tide would proceed westward and some ghastly Woking Workers Council would soon decide our fates. But by 1920, the conflict had receded into a vast and confusing Civil War, in which numerous factions, all of whom seemed to have their own colors, fought back and forth over the snows. The Greens, the Reds, the Whites, the Blacks—it was like a paints set had gone to war. Few truly appreciated that the British Empire, along with countless other countries, were also involved, sending munitions and soldiers to fight the Soviets and try to return the Whites to supremacy.

And fewer still would know that my old friend, the renowned Professor George Edward Challenger, played a part as well.

I must admit, I was surprised to receive the missive asking for my support, and to take up my role as the professor's chronicler, while I was interviewing the studio kings of Hollywood. Still, if there is one thing I know about Challenger, it is to be prepared for surprises.

So, I mailed off my Hollywood story, boarded a steamer from Los Angeles, and arrived in Vladivostok to meet with the professor again. I must admit, a great trepidation quickened my heart as I sailed. I'd covered the war in Europe,

the Rising in my own native Ireland, and various other theatres, and I was—
like many others—fed up with conflict.

But I would never see a war quite like what waited for me in Russia.

Strangely, I found Vladivostok, a half-frozen and dismal fishing town
located on the banks of the Pacific, occupied almost entirely by the same sort
of Americans that I had left in Hollywood. The American Expeditionary Force
for Siberia was going home, and the Army soldiers seemed determined to
wash away their defeats in Russia by drinking to excess and brawling in every
section of the city. I maneuvered carefully around several squabbles along dirt
paths stained with melted snow before arriving in a saloon with a bellowing
yak inscribed on the sign.

The professor waited for me at a table near the roaring fireplace, and greeted
me with a raised glass. A barrel-chested American soldier walked away from
him, gripping his arm and laughing delightedly. "Bested him at arm wrestling."
Challenger split his vast beard into a great smile. "Poor fellow. He had the strength,
I suppose—but didn't know how to use it." Then he patted the chair next to me.
"Sit down, Edward, my boy, and have something to warm your bones."

"Thanks." I readily accepted. The cold of that place seemed far more fearsome
than even the dead of winter in Northern England. The ice of Yorkshire might
chill, but it didn't seem to attack the body in the manner of the Russian cold.
My greatcoat, mittens, and wool cap made me comfortable enough, but it was
good to remove them. "You seem to be getting along well."

"The pursuit of science requires that I persevere and so persevere I must."
He poured himself a glass of something clear and acrid. "Vodka." He pushed
it toward me and poured another for himself. "Though it's the king's business
that brings me here."

"Government work?" I tried a sip. It seemed akin to drinking lightning. I
sputtered and shook in my seat, then fumbled for the canteen on my hip.

"Hah! That'll put some hair on your chest." The professor drained his
glass in a single gulp. For him, it might as well have been lemonade. "Yes, lad.
Military business. I served our government during the Great War, and so I
serve them here. Enemies of Western Civilization, these Bolsheviks. I shall do
whatever I can to hamper them."

"And what exactly is it the government would like you to do?"

He had refilled his glass, but paused. "Well, now that you mention it, I have no idea. I was instructed to arrive at this establishment every afternoon since my arrival two days ago, and wait for another agent of the crown, a man named Reilly. One of your countrymen, perhaps? So far, Reilly has yet to appear—leaving me to find my own amusements." He laughed heartily at that.

"So you have just been waiting?"

"I suppose I have. I don't mind it. I miss my dear Jessie, of course, and the cold is playing havoc on my joints. But this is an adventure, Edward, and I find myself having adventures less and less as I grow old."

And grow old he had. Veins of gray now slid through his great tangle of beard and he had swelled a little thicker around the middle. It seemed impossible. One might as well imagine a Viking God growing old as George Challenger—but there it was.

I looked past him—and my eyes settled on another fellow who didn't belong amongst the raucous Americans or drunken locals. This fellow wore a fine camelhair coat over a silken dark suit and vest, complete with Arrow Collar. A bowler hat rested on his lap. His eyes, nestled in a bloodless face, had the same shiny darkness as a tar pit.

He watched us for a few moments more and then stood and approached. "Professor Challenger." He settled down. "Good afternoon. Sidney Reilly, at your service." A curious accent. He had a Metropolitan Londoner's voice, but it was too composed and clipped. Only a trained journalistic ear would realize that it was false.

"Ah—Reilly!" Professor Challenger pumped his arm. "Good afternoon indeed! Please, take a seat." He motioned to me. "A friend of mine, Edward Malone. He's a newspaperman, but for being a member of that toxic brotherhood, he's a decent enough fellow. You may trust him with whatever you trust to me."

"A newspaperman?" Reilly drew out a silver cigarette case. "That may prove disadvantageous, in my profession."

"And what is your profession?" I inquired.

"Spy." He said it casually as his lighter snapped to life and burned the tip of his cigarette. "Though I'm not worried. If you prove troublesome, you can be dealt with." His hand vanished into his coat as he sucked in smoke.

I stared in alarm at this stark pronouncement of my being 'dealt with.' Reilly had threatened me with the same casualness that one might consider dealing with a problematic insect infestation in one's house. An annoyance that could easily be removed. Clearly, he was very capable in his job. Challenger glared darkly at Reilly, and squared his shoulders, like a father bear defending his cub. I could always trust that he would be on my side.

But Reilly had already set a carved ivory pipe on the scuffed wood of the table. "Do you know what this is, gentlemen?"

"That is a pipe," I said.

"Your simpleton ways are always refreshing, my dear boy." Challenger scooped up the pipe and examined it. "Ivory. Cyrillic characters carved upon it. A local craft, and there are no elephants in Siberia. I would guess it is mammoth ivory." He motioned to me with the pipe. "The locals find them, you know, the carcasses frozen and preserved. Most fascinating."

"Hmmm." Reilly took another drag on his cigarette. "Very astute, professor. But what if I told you that the ivory used to make that pipe did not come from a dead pachyderm, but from a living creature?"

"A survivor of the Ice Age?" The professor raised a bushy eyebrow. "Most would call you a madman. But young Malone would not be so quick to doubt the survival of prehistoric creatures"

"Maple-White Land." I whispered the name of that faraway place.

"I heard of it. The pterodactyl brought to London. Shrouded in secrecy, of course, but I have my sources." He took the pipe back from Professor Challenger. "It's why I requested your presence, sir. I think there is another such place, lost in the snows of Central Russia. Another Lost World."

"You did right to contact me," Challenger said. "And it is fortuitous that Malone came as well. You have here two of a handful of men who have visited such a place before."

"Where is this Lost World?" I inquired.

"I made inquiries amongst the peasants—the *muzhiks*, as they are called here. They speak of the Kingdom of Opona. The Golden Land. A paradise of plenty, ruled by a benevolent Tsar, who works to serve the common people."

"Reminiscent of Cockaigne, in our own country," Challenger said. "A dream of the peasants."

"Though it seems these peasants have stopped dreaming," I added. "And taken up arms."

Reilly remained impassive. "It is known more widely as Vyraj. A place where souls go upon their deaths. A land of the dead, where the living do not wander. Vyraj Valley. That is the name they have given this place."

"You know where it is? Or rumors of its location, perhaps?" Challenger sprang from his seat, his eyes ablaze. I had seen him like this before, animated with an inner fire for the longing of discovery. His hands gripped the table and I wondered if he would spring at Reilly and wrestle the information out of him.

The spy calmly smoked his cigarette. "You are certain? It promises to be very dangerous."

"The devil take the danger!" Challenger muttered. "I want those mammoths."

Reilly continued. "The Bolsheviks are gaining in strength in this part of the country, hunting down the last remnants of White resistance as the various allied expeditions return to their homelands. But there is one who is standing against them, and I think he might have arrived in Vyraj Valley itself." He shrugged. "Perhaps he wants to use mammoth ivory to fund his war. Or perhaps the valley, surrounded by thick mountains, makes an ideal redoubt."

"A last stand in a lost world," I murmured.

"What is the name of this Horatius of White Russia?" Challenger demanded.

"Baron Roman Von Ungern-Sternberg." A bit of a mouthful, to say the least. "I intend to make a study of this Baron Ungern and see if he truly has located Vyraj Valley. That's why I want you along." He stood, the cigarette burning between his fingers. "If you desire to accompany me into the hinterland, of course."

"By God, I desire nothing more!" Challenger sprang to his feet as well. "What preparations have you made, Mr. Reilly?"

"We'll take a train west, and go to an isolated station far from here. There, we'll have to rent a troika—a sleigh and three horses—and go to a place called the Leshy's Rest. From there, we'll see if we can locate the baron and his troops." His eyes settled on me. "You'll join us, Mr. Malone?"

"Where the professor goes, I'll follow," I replied.

"Loyal as a good hound—though about as intelligent." Challenger clapped me on the shoulder hard enough to make me wince. "However, Mr. Reilly, there is one question that has been burning in the back of my brain since your arrival. Your name—it makes one think of my friend's country. Dublin and County Cork and so forth. And yet, I detect nothing of the Gaelic about your physique or accent." He squinted. "Instead, you seem rather Semitic. Am I far off the mark, sir?"

In response, Reilly put his bowler hat on his head. "I'll see at you at the train station tomorrow morning. Goodbye, sir." And with that, he departed.

"Hmph!" Challenger plopped back in his seat. "A touchy subject."

"You are aware that there is a great persecution of Hebrews in these parts," I said. "Worsened perhaps, since the days of the Black Hundreds, by the chaos unleashed by Civil War."

"I care not for politics. It is a pastime for fools, largely practiced by fools, and devoted to the welfare or subjugation of fools." He poured his glass. "I suppose I had better pay my tab." Then his keen eyes settled on me. "Would you consider paying for a portion?"

I had learned long ago not to argue with G.E.C and so I paid without complaint.

The next morning, we began our journey into the hinterlands of Russia. A great rattling train, in some need of repair, trundled its way out over the snow. Professor Challenger, Sidney Reilly, myself, and our supplies, were nearly alone, apart from a few hulking bearded fellows, armed like the corsairs of old, who must be soldiers of fortune or dealers in arms seeking a closeness to the conflict. In terms of weaponry and supplies, Reilly had purchased Challenger and myself bolt-action rifles of Russian design, while he kept a magazine pistol hidden in his coat. A necessity, for the whole land was alive with bandits and deserters.

Were we in Siberia, the Transbaikal, or some other location on the great swath of Slavic land? I couldn't say. Reilly alone knew our destination: the Leshy's Rest. Challenger and I simply tucked our coats around us and waited.

By midmorning, we arrived at an isolated station. This place had a great crowd of refugees around it, and they surged up to the train as we departed. A true motley cross-section of Russia, from bearded peasants in fur hats to aristocrats with their pockets bulging from jewelry and whatever else they had managed to save. The train would be exceedingly crowded on the way back to Vladivostok.

Reilly procured a troika—a sleigh pulled by three horses—and we set off at once into the woods. Challenger himself took the reins. He would allow no one else to fulfill that role. "I don't trust either of you not to drive us straight into a snowbank or the side of a tree," he fumed. "Simply settle back and enjoy the view."

It was, at least, a picturesque view. We zoomed along through a great forest, maneuvering along on a narrow trail that wound amidst the boughs of the towering trees. The leaves had long since fallen away, leaving skeletal branches draped in snow. All the ice and frost caught sunlight streaming through the boughs, making the whole place gleam. Almost uncomfortable until Reilly supplied me with a pair of smoked glasses that helped shade my eyes. Mist hung about the branches and came from my throat, and there, in the silent undisturbed apart by the twittering of birds and the rustle of squirrels, we might have been the only souls on the face of a frozen earth.

There in the distance, lost amidst the treetops, a great mountain range loomed tall. A sheer wall of snow-covered rock, looking like a fairyland in the chill mist. Was that our destination?

Professor Challenger suddenly tugged at the reins and slowed the horses. The troika's runners went deep into the snow, casting up a great spray of sleet. We slid to a halt along the path. A moment later, I saw the reason for his delay.

"Good God." Challenger removed his wolf's fur ushanka. "Lord have mercy."

There, in a clearing next to the trail, a grim massacre had taken place. At least a score of men, women, and children lay crumpled on the snow, their gore mingling with the sleet. A few dead horses and donkeys accompanied of them. Currently, the ravens had swooped down from the trees to feed. At the edge, greater predators—a half-score hungry wolves—had gathered in a cluster. The wolves looked at us warily, apparently worried that we would steal their lunch.

I took hold of my rifle and leapt from the sleigh. "There may be survivors. Hurry!"

But Reilly remained where he stood. "We shouldn't tarry. Not in this part of the country. Leave them to the grave and let's ride on."

"Goddamn you, sir, have you no heart?" Challenger joined me. He hurried amongst the dead, keeping his rifle trained on the wolves. "Bullet wounds. The work of blades." And they had been used fearfully well. "By their somber dress and ear locks, I judge these to be your fellow Hebrews, Mr. Reilly. Will you not assist your countrymen?"

He remained still. "I have no countrymen."

I stepped gingerly around the body of an elderly fellow, his head nearly separated by a Cossack's blade, and faced the wolves. "Who could have done this?"

"Baron Ungern, perhaps. I've heard rumors about him." Reilly nodded toward the wolves. "They follow him around, they say. The packs, knowing that he will leave a trail of bodies and bones wherever his armies go. That he always feeds the wolves."

"Rumors." I shuddered. "That can't be true."

I couldn't consider that the fellow we were going to see was the sort of monster who ordered his cavalrymen to fall upon innocent people like demons.

A slight groan came from someone near the edge of the clearing. A survivor? "Professor, see to the wolves." I slung my rifle over my back and hurried over.

"I'll do better than that." Challenger took aim. "I'll scatter them."

Reilly leapt down from the wagon. "Professor, I beg of you, do not—"

But Challenger had already fired. The rifle thundered, sending the pack of wolves darting away. The ravens lifted off as well, fluttering skyward in a great black mass. The leaves swayed a little as the gunshot echoed over the forest.

"Now, our presence will be known." Reilly glared at us. "We must get back to the road."

I ignored him. Instead, I went to the edge and spotted a little movement. A young woman, with copper-colored hair, huddled against a fallen log. I hurried to her and Challenger did the same. She panicked, letting out a shout and rolling over—but she lacked the strength to make good an escape. She faced us, eyes wide with terror. She was perhaps in her early twenties and, judging by the hair-color of the corpses around her, the only survivor of a family of five.

"Madam, I assure you, we mean no harm." I addressed her in my best Russian and she seemed to understand. "We are travelers. Englishmen." I motioned to the sleigh. "We'll get you out of here. I promise."

"What—what are you doing here?" She spoke Yiddish, but was able to make herself understood.

"And see to your arm," Challenger said. "Looks broken."

"Leave her!" Reilly called again, shouting from the wagon. "Let her walk to the train station on foot. We must not delay."

"You heartless fiend!" Challenger roared back. "You would condemn a wounded woman—the same age as my daughter perhaps—to a cold death! I care not about the consequences. We are staying put and helping her."

"Professor, please." I put a hand on his shoulder. "You're frightening the girl."

He faced her and lowered his head. "My apologies." His Russian came flawlessly and his tone was amazingly gentle—the polar opposite of his usual manner. It was quite a thing to see. "I had no intention of adding to your distress." He offered his hand. "I'll have my friend here make a fire while I look at your arm." He hesitated. "May I ask you, what is your name?"

She shuddered a final time. "Esther." Then she looked below her at the bodies of her parents and two siblings—she was the eldest—and the tears ran silently down her cheeks.

"A fine name." Professor Challenger put a hand on her shoulder and helped her up. "I wish we could bury them. I fear the ground is too hard—and if we started digging graves, I think we should never stop." He nodded toward me. "See about making a fire. We'll do what we can."

I took a hatchet from the troika and cut up a mass of dead branches to make the fuel. Soon enough, we had a merry blaze going. Challenger worked tirelessly to bind Esther's arm and crafted a sling for her as well. We gave her one of our spare coats, and draped it over her thin shoulders.

She spoke little, wincing occasionally as Challenger worked. He supplied her with a bottle of vodka, and bade her to sip it for the pain. After he had finished, he took a sip himself before joining me. "I'd like her to accompany us to Vyraj Valley. I think she will be safer in our company than on the roads."

Reilly snorted. "Are you asking for my opinion, professor? You have ignored it entirely. I see no reason why I should waste my breath."

"Your opinions are inhuman and cruel!" Challenger bellowed.

"And your mission of charity—pointless in the face of the vast slaughter overtaking Russia—has just placed us all in needless danger."

"Gentlemen, please—" I attempted to stop the quarreling duo. Perhaps a foolhardy pursuit. Then, Esther began to rock back and forth and emit words in a language I did not know. Not Russian or Yiddish. More silent tears trickled down her freckled cheeks as the words tumbled from her lips. "What is she doing?"

"The Mourner's Kaddish," Reilly explained. "A prayer for the dead."

"So, you do indeed share a heritage." Challenger looked delighted, as if he had just found the one piece of evidence that would allow him to win some scientific debate against a hated rival. "I knew it. And yet, you ignored them and urged us to ride on."

"If I concerned myself with small matters, if I clung to the old ways, like they did—" He motioned to the corpses. "Then perhaps I would join them. Then again, I may join them anyway."

"What the devil are you talking about?" I asked.

Reilly pointed down the road as he came to his feet. "I'll need you to trust me—even if you haven't already. We're about to have company."

The drumming of hooves and the turning of wheels on snow resounded down the road. A ragtag cavalry column emerged, coming through the forest and heading straight for us. A dozen horsemen emerged first, clad in rumpled, olive-green uniforms and cartridge belts. Carbines and cavalry sabers at their sides. Behind them came a trio of strange conveyances. Tachankas— an example of Ukrainian ingenuity that put a machine gun in the back of a rattling wagon. Currently, those machine guns were trained on us.

"Whites?" I asked.

"Reds." Reilly grimaced and went to the center of the road, his hands raised. Now, I could make out the details of their uniforms. Red stars and the Sickles and Hammers, emblazoned on their greatcoats and garments. Bolsheviks indeed.

I glanced at Challenger, who looked at his rifle, now leaning against our sleigh.

"If only we had Lord John with us now," he muttered.

Indeed. Lord John Roxton, master hunter and veteran soldier, was known as the Flail of the Lord on three continents. Even in the trenches, he had flourished. He would know what to do. Unfortunately, he was presently engaged elsewhere. Professor Challenger and myself would have to suffice.

The column came to a stop. The ranks of these communist cavaliers parted and a woman rode to their head. A sort of Bolshevik Joan of Arc. She wore a ragged uniform and a peaked cap marked with a scarlet star, her hair shaved almost down to the scalp. A scar crossed her pale face, running from chin to the tip of her nose. Her hand dropped to the revolver on her belt as she looked us over.

"What are you doing here?" She spoke a clipped Russian. "I am Captain

...a ragtag cavalry column emerged...

Nadia Nevskaya of the Red Army, Seventh Battalion of the People's Mounted Guards." It reminded me of being under the gaze of a stern governess after I had neglected my studies. No excuse came to mind. None would suffice.

Professor Challenger walked past me and responded. "Travelers, ma'am. Simple travelers, traversing this snowy region. We're bound for the Leshy's Rest. Do you know it?"

"We have our made our camp there." She leaned on her saddle horn. "Englishmen?"

"A Scot, actually. Professor George Edward Challenger is my name." He patted my arm. "And an Irishman. Edward Malone." Behind him, Esther had come to her feet. She gripped her wounded arm. "We found the woman there, amongst the dead. And then there's—"

"Captain." Reilly brushed past Challenger and approached Nevskaya. He drew out a red notebook and held it in her hand. "I am Semyon Reznov, counter-intelligence agent." He smiled, like he had made the winning move in a Chess game. "Cheka."

The Cheka—the feared secret police of the revolution.

"What?" Challenger stared in horror at Reilly. "You blackguard! Judas!"

"He's—he's an intelligence officer with the—" But I stopped. If I told this Soviet soldier that Reilly was an agent of British intelligence, what would she think toward the professor and myself? Doubtlessly, we would be just as guilty as he.

Still, it was a cruel business. Reilly appeared to be sacrificing us both to save his own skin.

Reilly continued, ignoring us both. "Captain, I infiltrated the ranks of the foreigner invaders. These two are counter-revolutionary agents, sent to thwart the will of the people." He spoke the same rapid Russian as Captain Nevskaya, and I found it difficult to understand all the Marxist language packed into his words. "I advise you to capture them both and allow me to oversee their interrogation."

"Poppycock!" Challenger bellowed. "This backstabbing brute is nothing but a snake."

"Please." Esther drew closer to him. "They are good people, madam."

"Enough." Captain Nevskaya rested her hands on her saddle horn. "You. Englishmen. Get on your troika." He glared at Esther. "Your Jew friend can go with you." Her men had already ridden about the wagon. One Soviet giant descended from his saddle and snatched away our rifles, then went through our supplies in search of any more weapons. "Try and ride off and we'll cut you down." She motioned to the tachankas, with their machine guns. "You wanted to see Leshy's Rest, don't you? You will."

Challenger looked like he wanted to launch himself at the Soviets and put his fists to use. I knew how frequently he resorted to fisticuffs, but he'd be shot if he tried. I put my hand on his shoulder. "We must play their game, professor. For now."

He snorted. "Right, right." Then he offered his hand to Esther. "Shall we?"

She bobbed her head weakly and we all settled back onto the sleigh.

Reilly still remained on the snow. "Captain, may I trouble you for a horse?"

She nodded and motioned to her men. A slope-shouldered Bolshevik led out a swaybacked mare without a rider. "You may take Evgeni's horse. Maybe it will do you better than it did him."

"Wonderful." He pulled himself into the saddle and took the reins—a little awkwardly perhaps, but he managed. Then he glanced back at the wagon. His eyes met mine. He winked.

Was that merely a twitch or a shiver? Or notification that he had some gambit prepared? Either way, it didn't make me feel much better as the entire procession set out once again, down the snowy trail and toward Leshy's Rest.

The Bolsheviks had transformed the Leshy's Rest into a singularly miserable and desolate armed camp. They had a few tents in a ragged circle, a broken armored car, a stockade of fallen logs taken from the forest, and a few flickering cookfires.

But next to it, the Vyraj Valley waited. The great rock walls, thick and tall as those of cathedral, stretched up into the mist. The stone, smeared with ice, appeared to present a challenge for even the most capable mountaineer. However, another passage—a sort of long canyon—provided some passage. Perhaps a coach and a team of horses could make their way through the pass and enter the Valley.

To see the wonders that waited within.

Captain Nevskaya rode next to the sleigh as we entered the center of her encampment. "Counter-revolutionary forces have gathered there. Baron Ungern. The Bloody White Baron."

Esther spat into the snow. "A monster! He attacked my people."

"A true butcher." Nevskaya stared at the pass. "Remnants of the Tsar's army. They've been attacking patrols through this part of the country for months. We've been sent to finish them." She swung down from the saddle. "Challenger, Malone—I think you will be our scouts."

"Into the valley?" I asked.

"*Nyet.*" Nevskaya pointed. "Into the cave."

A dark gash, a cut in the stone, lay next to the encampment. Darkness filled the cave, like some slanting mouth that would welcome us hungrily into the belly beyond. I had no desire to enter that cave. The darkness waited to consume me completely and a low shudder burned out in the bottom of my belly. Our ancestors feared the dark for good reason. Who knew what waited inside?

"We have lost two men to something—something in that cave." Nevskaya looked at the mountain walls. "Vyraj. The land of the dead. Who knows what waits there?" She faced Challenger and myself. "You will do a service for the Motherland. Find out what's inside. What is killing my men."

"No." Esther darted closer to Nevskaya. "Please—they do not deserve that. The Professor, Malone—they are good men."

"They are enemies of the revolution." Nevskaya remained unmoved. "They go into the cave."

Reilly had dismounted and walked closer. He stepped next to Challenger, a sudden sneer appearing on his usually impassive face. "You are frightened, professor?"

"Frightened? Never." He folded his massive arms. "Compared to the dangers I've faced, Mr. Reilly—or Reznov as you now call yourself—a darkened cave inhabited by a monster is a mere stroll in a verdant park."

"Oh, I doubt that sincerely, sir." Reilly wagged his finger at Challenger. "For what are you but a rotten little boy, blathering away at the public to get their interest in your youthful pranks?" He placed an oily grin on his face. "And all little boys fear the dark."

Now, Challenger did launch himself at Reilly. He emitted a wordless, roaring cry and tackled him. They went to the snow together. "Fiend!" Challenger swung his fists down, scoring an excellent right hook against Reilly's cheek. "Rat! I'll tear you in half and—"

The Bolsheviks gave him no chance to do more damage. They swarmed around Challenger—it took six of them, but they managed—and pulled him free from Reilly. They plopped Challenger onto the snow, next to me, where he glowered and snarled hatefully. Only a trio of bayonets, pointed right at his chest, held him back from attacking Reilly once more.

Reilly returned to his feet and brushed snow from his coat. He moved next to Esther, took her good arm, and led her away—looking like nothing so much as a gent and his best girl going for a stroll.

Captain Nevskaya removed her peaked cap. "I almost fear for what's in the cave. Now, you have wasted enough time. Go."

I offered my hand to Challenger. "Come on, professor. Better we face whatever is in that cave then deal with a Bolshevik firing squad. We have a chance."

He adjusted his coat and paused. A sudden smile on his beard. "I suppose we do. Come on."

The Soviet soldiers escorted us to the mouth of the cave. Challenger and I crossed the snow slowly—two condemned men, going to the gallows. Perhaps the Bolshevik bullets would be better than whatever waited in the darkness. A faster death, at least. I had to crouch low to avoid the stone ceiling of the cave mouth. Challenger, a bigger fellow than me, slid to the side. We went down crab fashion, sliding slightly on the gravel and frost, before reaching the cave floor.

Darkness, apart from the slit above that had been our entrance. Bitingly cold, even though not much snow entered this place. "Hold on." Challenger drew his lighter and flashed it to life. "There we are. See if you can find some dry branches, lad. Anything that burns would be most useful."

We busied ourselves around the cave floor. I struck a match as well, increasing the circle of illumination. Thankfully, we did find a dead branch and some matching leaves. Challenger sacrificed his scarf for binding and soon enough, a makeshift torch blazed in each of our hands. That sent light all around this chamber—an antechamber, as we revealed.

Another passage led further into the dark. "Shall we?" I asked.

Professor Challenger snorted. "Yes. Hold on a moment. There's some odd weight in my coat pocket and—" He grinned, his bright white teeth shimmering in the torchlight and making him look even more like some pagan idol. "Cunning Reilly! Clever, duplicitous, and heroic."

"What?" I could hardly believe it. "But he betrayed us—"

"I thought he did. But look at this." Challenger drew out the magazine pistol. "He stuffed it into my pocket during our little scuffle back there."

"So he did care about saving his skin, but seems willing to try and save ours as well." I considered this new development. "Is he really on our side?"

"He's on one side—his own. But he must think he is in a better position if we are armed and alive than not." Challenger pointed to the tunnel ahead. "I'll lead, Malone, with pistol at the ready."

An automatic pistol. I didn't know many bullets it carried, but they were our only defense. The gun's presence didn't make me feel much better.

We continued in silence through the cave, stumbling over indentations in the stone floor. The tunnel swerved and shifted, broken by stalactites and stalagmites stretching up like great teeth. I patted one stone and the cold went through my mittens. This was an ancient place, formed over eons, and it felt as if human feet had no business crossing it.

Something crunched under my boot. "Ah!" I looked down. Bones—a lean stretch of yellowed bone which had fallen from a small pile of them gathered in an alcove. "Challenger, look at this." I hoisted up my torch, shining light at the mass of bones.

Professor Challenger crouched down and examined them. "An ossuary." He picked up one. "That jawbone—from a deer, perhaps. Though I cannot recognize the type." Then his light shone on a human skull. His eyes opened—not in horror, but in deeper interest. "Pass that to me, my boy. I want a closer look."

"The skull?"

"No, the smoking jacket. Of course, the skull, you utter dunce!"

I clutched the skull with shaking fingers and passed it to him. "A man-eating monster left that," I muttered.

Challenger hoisted it up. "Not *man*-eating. Look, you have as much intelligence as an earthworm, but even you know what a human skull looks like." He traced his fingers along the top. "This is not that. The brow is too pronounced." Indeed, the space above the eyeholes did seem remarkably thick. "This skull is akin to those found in the Neander Valley in 1856. In short, it belonged to a Neanderthal. They were a simple people. They made tools, occupied caves in Europe—and vanished upon the arrival of our species. Never did the Neanderthals make grand inventions or explore the globe."

Nor did they populate the planet, and fill it up with motorcars. And, most recently, the trenches of the Great War.

My mind raced. "Is it, by chance, ancient?"

"This skull appears to be modern, my boy."

"Ah." I examined that pronounced ridge and those hollow sockets. "The Neanderthals. Were they simple animalistic creatures like those we encountered in Maple-White Land?"

"A matter of speculation," Challenger explained. "For our race has not encountered a Neanderthal in millennia. But we have other concerns. Namely, what manner of beast put this skull here?"

That's when we heard the roar—nearly next to us. I spun around and hoisted my torch, and it was only that light which saved us.

A monster crouched on a rocky ledge, coiled up and ready to spring. Thick shoulders covered in tawny fur, now rendered shadowy in the darkness. Glowering, bright green cat eyes and lips curled back to reveal a mouth full of terrible teeth. Two massive fangs in particular, each seemingly as big as Bowie knives, reaching down and slick with saliva.

Gazing at this monstrosity, I felt like the mouse when the cat approached.

Professor Challenger hurled the skull at the tiger, just as it pounced, and then grabbed my arm. We ran down the tunnel, claws clicking on the stone behind us. "A bloody saber-tooth tiger!" He spun his pistol around and fired blind. The automatic thundered, the boom echoing across the stone and making my ears ache. "What a miraculous find!"

A miraculous find that would perhaps devour us all. We kept running, dashing down the tunnel as Challenger unloaded the remaining bullets in his pistol. The muzzle flash blared bright, enough to make my eyes blink and turn the world yellow before it succumbed to flickering darkness once more. I banged my arms and legs into the stone, struck my head on a low ceiling, and still stumbled on.

Anything but to look at that predator behind me and to feel the same terror of our ancestors: the knowledge that a powerful beast, fanged and hungry, crept behind you and was about to bury its saber-teeth in your back.

Up ahead, we saw the slit leading back into the fresh air. The wind had increased, and a screen of swirling ice and wind danced in front of the entrance. The hazy little blizzard cast up great deals of snow, sending the mist in wild swirls. It was like looking through a telescope wrapped in gossamer.

I squinted, trying to make out what was happening. Gunfire sounded, and men shouted and screamed. A machine gun gave off a burst before falling silent.

It sounded like an avalanche and a battle all in one.

"Should we risk it?" I called to Challenger.

"Better that than face the saber-tooth." He glared at his empty pistol. "Come on!"

We made it to the cave mouth and scrambled over. Sliding over the stone and back onto the snowy floor of the Soviet encampment. Malone and I struggled to catch our breath as we stared at the mist and chaos now enveloping the Leshy's Rest.

It was the purest example of the madness of war as I have ever seen—akin to the more orderly battles on the Western Front only in the fact that there appeared to be two sides fighting each other. The Soviets dashed about, firing their rifles madly into the mist and unable to make a firing line or form any kind of defense. All around them, the enemy rode. Wild horsemen, bearing great fur cloaks and firing from their saddle or swinging down lethal curved sabers and slaughtering their foes. Blood sprayed brilliant red across the snow, casting crimson lines against the frost and the tents as the enemy cavalrymen did their grim work.

Who were these attackers? I tried to catch a good look, but the mist, kicked-up frost, and sheer speed of their horsemanship left me vexed. They bore a mix of Russian and Mongolian fur hats, with wild moustaches and beards and blazing eyes. Strange symbols—from the Double-Headed Russian Eagle to snarling ancient gods—on badges on their cross belts and bandoliers.

But that wasn't all. A tachanka rattled past us, the crew on the back trying to swing around the mounted machine gun to fire at the attackers. Then, a giant, furred shape burst out of the mist. I caught a glimpse of an elephantine bulk, great ivory tusks that caught the low sunlight, and massive pillar-like legs clad in dark fur. A trunk struck down like a great furry serpent, grabbed the unfortunate gunner, hauled him from his seat, and tossed him screaming into the distance. Then, the beast rammed its tusks and bulk into the wagon and smashed it into matchwood.

Who was the winner of this brutal skirmish? It seemed hard to figure out what was even occurring, but I had to judge that it was the attackers. The Soviets couldn't gather together to mount a defense. Not against the pounding hooves, flashing sabers, and apparent war elephants used so expertly by the opposite side—whoever they might be.

Professor Challenger watched the slaughter with a deranged awe. He pointed to the dark shape, now vanishing into the mist. "Mammoths. Wooly mammoths." He smiled once again. "Another Maple-White Land! Another lost world!"

"And it seems just as dangerous as the first." I took his arm. "We must find some manner of escape."

"Malone!" A familiar voice, almost lost in the chaos. Esther. She came riding out of the mist on our sleigh, Reilly next to her. The spy had a rifle in his hand, occasionally firing at a pursuer. Esther struggled with the reins, but managed to bring the conveyance to a halt before us. The horses reared up and whickered in their harness, doubtlessly as terrified by the proceedings as we were.

Reilly leaned down and offered his hand. "Come aboard. Hurry!"

Professor Challenger responded by grabbing me, his hands around my waist, and tossing me right into the back of the sleigh as if I were a sack of meal. I tumbled against the seat and lay in a tangle next to Reilly.

Another of those great lumbering shapes neared us. Breaking into a charge and leaving the mist. A trumpet left its trunk, echoing across the stones in a terrible battle cry. It loomed above us, the curved tusks like some bizarre raised executioner's axe. Above the round head of the mammoth, a sort of howdah of animal skins waited, bearing a flag emblazoned with both the Romanov seal and a golden banner of an unknown Eastern symbol. Men in ragged uniforms served as mahouts, and directed the great beast forward.

"Go!" Challenger cried, breaking into a run. "I'll jump aboard!"

Esther cracked the reins and the sleigh set off. Challenger ran along. I offered my hand and he took it. Reilly took his shoulder. We got him up, his legs kicking in the air for a few moments, before we got him over the railing and safely into the troika.

"There!" Reilly pointed ahead, to the gap in the mountain walls. "Into the valley."

"Okay." Esther twisted her good arm, and the horses galloped to the side. We spun around the edge of the mountain pass, momentum lifting one set of runners entirely into the air, before crashing down and resuming our speedy journey. They kept galloping hard, and we slid over the frosted floor. Massive stone walls on both sides. Icy mist ahead. Chaos and raging battle behind us.

But, for now, we were safe.

"Who were they?" Challenger asked. "Our attackers? Those expert horsemen and mammoth-riders?"

"The Baron's men," Esther said.

Baron Roman Von Ungern-Sternberg's desperadoes. The men who were making their final stand against the Bolsheviks, and who had butchered her family.

I was glad we had not stayed to greet them.

Challenger settled back in his seat. "Dear God, I would kill for a cigarette."

Reilly handed him his silver case. "There you are."

"You have my gratitude, sir." The professor took out a coffin nail and lit it. "And my apologies. Insulting me like that, earning my rage so that you could slip me the pistol. It was a very cunning gambit. Very cunning indeed. And pretending to switch sides, to go from an agent of the crown to an agent of Lenin? That was a genius lie indeed."

The spy shrugged and said nothing. Had it been a lie? Perhaps he didn't want to say. "You should thank Esther." He indicated the young woman currently doing her best to drive the sleigh.

"Oh?" I asked.

"Yes. I wished to take the sleigh, pick her up, and drive away. She insisted on your rescue."

I offered my hand and she clasped it. "I rather thought we would be the gallant heroes saving you, but it appears to be the other way around."

"Perhaps." She offered me a quick smile. "But do you know where we're going?"

"Vyraj Valley, my dear girl," Challenger replied. "The land of the dead."

And with such prehistoric monsters as the saber-tooth tiger and that mammoth running about, its title seemed very apropos indeed.

Reilly handed him the silver case.

By the afternoon, we had left the mountain pass completely and entered Vyraj Valley itself. And what a sight it was! A grand collection of frozen meadows, rolling hills, and great forests. Everywhere, set along the sides, the towering mountain walls stretching up into the heavens. Wherever you cared to look, those great stones loomed magnificently in the distance. I had, during my time in California, paid a visit to the Yosemite Valley in California, and this place had a similar grandeur, only covered in endless ice.

Challenger removed his cap as he stared around, Esther looked about with wide eyes, and I felt my pulse quicken. Even Reilly seemed impressed.

But the true wonder came a few moments later, when we passed the first set of Vyraj Valley's residents. A half-frozen field stretched out past an icy forest, sparse tundra grass rearing up in bluish clumps amongst the ice and jagged stumps of stone. There, grazing on the vegetation, a host of creatures that seemed to have stepped in from a dreamland of the African savannah. They had the rotund bodies, angular faces, and large horns of rhinos, but were completely covered in dense, shaggy fur.

The herd of these oddities clopped at the grass, the males occasionally giving their heads a shake to wave their horns in the air. Little calves gamboled about the thick legs of their parents, emitting merry bleats as they played on the grass. A few of them raised their heads and watched us warily, misty breath spraying about their muzzles.

"The Behemoth," Esther exclaimed. "From the Torah. The creature that appears at the end of time."

"Not quite, my dear." Challenger waved toward the rhinos with his smoldering cigarette. "I believe they are Wooly Rhinos, a smaller contemporary of the mammoths. They once populated primeval Europe as their descendants do to the plains of Africa today." He tapped my shoulder and pointed. "And see there! Creatures from your own homeland, Malone!"

Sure enough, a herd of Irish Elk had emerged from the forest to join the wooly rhinos in their grazing. These great beasts towered over their modern versions, and the bucks had a set of horns so absurdly huge that they might have been added by an enthusiastic child. The great elk sniffed in our direction before settling down to graze.

To see these magnificent creatures, breathing the air and strutting about, left me nearly tongue-tied with amazement. The size, the strangeness, the beauty: they had all been seen by human eyes only in the distant past before vanishing—except that here, in the Vyraj Valley, they remained. This truly was an afterlife, where the dead lived.

"Like Maple-White Land," I said.

"Maple-White Land indeed." Challenger patted Esther. "Take the reins. We have to keep moving."

Our sleigh rattled along, skirting the edge of the grazing lands. We worked our way along the side, giving the ancient animals a wide berth, and then neared a set of hills leading to the greater mountains in the distance. It proved difficult, with jagged spurs of dark stone rearing up from the steepening snow. Challenger and I hopped out and took the reins of the horses, helping them navigate the difficult terrain. Reilly went behind us, his rifle raised, while Esther—still weak from her ordeal in the woods—rode on the top.

We reached the peak of the first hill—and encountered another set of the valley's occupants.

They burst out from behind an oblong stone, unleashing a chorus of hoots and snarls and brandishing simple spears and war clubs. Perhaps a dozen in number and all armed. All of them wore ragged garments of various furs, including the shaggy exteriors of mammoths, stitched together in a great capes and tunics. Their hair, in reds, browns, and blondes, had something of the Scandinavian about it, and their waving weaponry made me feel like my Irish ancestors had when they spotted the dragon-headed ships of the Vikings cruising in for a raid.

But all of them had thick limbs and thick eyebrows, with broad noses and wide cheeks. Matching the skull which we had found in the saber-tooth's cave.

They were clearly Neanderthals.

Reilly swung into action, taking his rifle and aiming it at this war party. "Professor, move back." He kept the long arm steady as the hooting band advanced.

"Don't you shoot, Reilly!" Challenger waved his thick hands at the spy. "You'll get one or two of them before they rush us and put those spears to use."

"Or they'll run?" I suggested. "Having never faced firearms before?"

"Baron Ungern's settled in this place, remember? From what we've seen, he loves guns dearly. The Neanderthals are doubtlessly all too familiar. But I doubt this is a war party. They are too few, and too lightly armed. They're simply hunters." Challenger dropped the reins of the horse and approached the Neanderthals. "Easy there…easy. We mean no harm."

He spread his hands out, showing his palms. For humans, it was a universal symbol of peace, understood by all humans as a gesture of good will. Then again, these Neanderthals were not human. Some of them lowered their spears slightly and glanced at each other. They talked amongst each other, their voices bizarrely high-pitched and lilting. It was like being attacked by some savage children's choir.

"Yes, you see? Our intentions are entirely peaceful." Challenger took another step closer, moving toward the cluster. "We are explorers, yes? We've traveled to your valley, to study you, and the great beasts that dwell here, and—"

He slipped on the snow and caught himself—but lunged slightly toward the hunting party.

Having experienced one of the professor's lunges, I was not surprised that it caused no small amount of consternation amongst the Neanderthals. They hooted and called out in their birdsong voices, and brandished their weapons again.

Then, another voice joined the cacophony. A singing voice. "*Schlof mayn kind, mayn treyst, mayn scheyner...*" Esther's voice. Her song had the simple tune and quiet reassurance of a lullaby, sung in Yiddish. She had descended from the sleigh and walked towards the Neanderthals, still singing. Her words echoed over the cold slope, wafting their way past the jagged, protruding stones. Perhaps it was always a sad melody, or perhaps Esther's voice just made it sad.

The Neanderthals watched her approach and listened. Gradually, their frenzied talk faded. They lowered their spears. Clearly, they judged that anything that could sing in this calm manner could not be a threat.

I glanced at Reilly. He stared into the distance, blinking rapidly. The only change in his impassive expression. Had he heard this lullaby when he was growing up? Perhaps the memory still lingered, despite his long career in espionage.

Esther walked down from the sleigh as she sang and came to the Neanderthal at the head of their war party. She looked him over. "Did you like it? My father used to sing it to my baby brother. Both gone now. Perhaps the song is all I have." She offered her good hand. "Do you have a name? I'm Esther, yes?" She pointed to herself. "Esther. And you?"

He answered in his singsong high-pitched way, giving a very long name indeed. It might have been a full paragraph.

"Look at the fellow's moustache." Challenger pointed. "Do you know who that looks like?"

"By God, you're right!" The small toothbrush moustache, standing our dark and shaggy on his upper lip. Very odd, and matched by a bit more beard, but the resemblance of facial hair was indeed very similar to one of the most famous popular motion picture stars of the age. "It's Chaplin."

"Who?" Esther asked.

"Charlie Chaplin," Reilly explained. "The funny man in the Moving Pictures."

"Charlie." Esther nodded. "Shall we call you 'Charlie'?" She pointed to him.

Our newly christened Neanderthal nodded. "Charlie. Hmmm." He faced his friends. "Charlie!" They all nodded their agreement, a few clapping their hands or jabbing their spears into the snow to make enthusiastic crunching noises. Then Charlie looked back at us. "You. Come. Us."

Speaking a butchered, but still somewhat acceptable Russian.

"What?" Esther stepped back. "But how do you know—"

"Come. See Kahn." Charlie pointed back over the hills, toward the mountain.

"Kahn?" Challenger asked. "What the devil does he mean?"

"I don't know any more than you do," Reilly replied.

That's when Charlie's cloak shifted, and revealed a medal placed on the fur. An old tin affair, dented and rusted. But the double-headed eagle of the Tsar remained.

Baron Ungern had been here for some time, sending out his sorties like the ones who had attacked Esther's family, and solidifying his power. He had either conquered, enslaved, or earned the loyalty of the Neanderthals. Now, they were his servants, and we had no choice but comply to their demands— however nicely they were put.

Esther looked back at Challenger. He motioned for her to join him. "No need to worry, my dear. I assure you, Mr. Malone and I won't let anything happen to you. We'll speak to this Baron Ungern and be on our way."

"And that's what we wanted to do anyway, isn't it?" I asked Reilly. "To judge if he needs British support for the war against the Bolsheviks?"

"Yes." Reilly slung his rifle over his back. "Those are my orders. It will be nice to see them carried out."

We all returned to the sleigh. The Neanderthals walked alongside us, Charlie showing us the way down the hills and toward the mountain in the distance. What would Ungern be like? We had seen his handiwork, but at least he was no Bolshevik. Still, I dreaded what waited for us at the end of the trail. An underworld needed a monarch, after all. Perhaps we were going to see the devil himself.

We departed the hills and reached a stretch of flat land, all around a towering lump of stone—the mountain, like the center of a sundial, in the middle of the Vyraj Valley. This was where Baron Roman Von Ungern-Sternberg had made his camp. He had a small stockade around the perimeter, followed by rows of tents and a few lean-tos and shacks made from animal skins, wood, and stone. Bonfires crackled continuously, bathing everything in a haze of smoke and firelight. Charlie and his Neanderthal scouts led us past these defenses and tents and straight for the mountain in the middle.

The soldiers of the baron lounged about the campsite, drinking, laughing, and playing cards. They stopped to watch us, glaring at us from below fur hats and peaked caps. A motley collection of warriors. Tartars, Poles, Russians, Cossacks, Mongolians—all wearing their medallions and badges and bearing swords. A few tossed snowballs at Charlie, and laughed as he screeched and shook his spear at them. Esther drew closer to me as the horses trotted their way to the middle of the camp. Her family's killers had to be here.

A few other Neanderthals moved about, bringing chunks of meat to the waiting soldiers. The conquered, now serving as slaves.

That wasn't the only example of the locals being tamed. Close to the mountain, Baron Ungern's men had constructed a giant corral, using entire trees as the beams. Inside, a herd of mammoths huddled together. They appeared to have at least two or three families there, the calves huddling against the thick, hairy legs of their parents. Their tusks jabbed outward, useless as protection against their captors. Several mammoths still bore the howdahs that had carried their riders into battle.

It was not a pleasant thing, to see those great beasts held captive. They belonged free, dashing about in the cold wilderness. But Baron Ungern doubtlessly saw them only as engines of war, and treated the mammoths accordingly.

Charlie reached the foot of the mountain. A stony pathway led up, winding in switchbacks up the mountain and passing numerous cave entrances. We would have to leave the troika, but had little choice. I offered my hand to Esther, but she scrambled down herself—huddled in her borrowed coat and shivering madly. Doubtlessly terrified of what we would find at the top.

We traveled up the slope, passing more torches and fires that shone lights into the caves. There, the Neanderthal families huddled. We caught glimpses of walls covered with centuries of cave paintings, the etchings spindly and somewhat resembling those works of the modernists that so shocked the art world. The Neanderthals themselves watched us, all huddled in skins and looking like prisoners in their own homes.

That was what Baron Ungern had made them.

Banners dangled along the rocks or fluttered from flagpoles sat on the edges, showing a multitude of bizarre symbols. The double-headed Romanov eagle was in attendance, but also some snarling toothy demon, perhaps Tibetan in origin, while another showed a set of crossed swords. Cossack guards waited at regular intervals, working on pipes while they shouldered their rifles. They followed closely behind us as we neared a large chamber further up the slope—forming a silent guard.

Reilly still had his rifle, but I doubted it would do much good. These

Cossacks seemed more fearsome than the Neanderthals, and far outnumbered us. If he fired, we were all finished. He knew it too and simply walked ahead, taking everything in.

The baron was supposed to be our ally, after all.

Then, we reached a cave in the center, which Baron Roman Von Ungern-Sternberg had turned into his throne room. Two great firepits burned in both corners, causing light to flash across the fine furnishings and carpet that he had doubtlessly imported from some great dacha further west. He even had a chandelier dangling from the cave ceiling. Countless weapons leaned against the walls. Rifles, swords, machine guns, and an assortment of polearms, all waited to be used.

There, seated on the gilded chair near the fires, sat the baron himself. For such a fearsome figure, he seemed strangely small—nearly draped in a golden robe bedecked with various medals, and a curved Mongolian sword with a shimmering hilt at his waist. Wild, dark hair and a reddish moustache and goatee rested under eyes that looked constantly to the horizon with an expression of burning hatred.

A half-dozen Cossack guards lounged in his apartment behind him, and that wasn't all. The biggest bear I have ever seen, a true monster curled up like a furry mountain by the dresser and chest of drawers. A chain around its throat went into a rung wedged in the cave wall.

For a few moments, the baron didn't appear to notice us. Then, he sucked in breath and rose slowly, pushing himself up from his chair, before turning around and staring at us. He stumbled a little before taking us in. "Who are you?" He shouted the sudden exclamation. "Bolshevik spies? Judeo-Bolsheviks, seeking my destruction?" He pulled his sword, letting the fading sunlight catch the blade. "I know how to deal with spies."

Challenger glowered back. "Put that sword away, sir, or I'll put it somewhere unpleasant."

"What?" Baron Ungern stomped toward us. "I shall take your head. I will let the crows pick it clean. Your death will be a lesson to all who—"

"We're not Bolsheviks!" I drew out my passport. Perhaps that would persuade him—if a madman can be persuadable. "I am Edward Malone, a reporter. This is Professor George Edward Challenger, a scholar of natural history. And these are—our associates." I thought it wise not to mention Reilly's profession, or Esther's identity. "We were sent by the British government to see about possible help. Possible support for your men, sir. Against the Bolsheviks."

"Against the Bolsheviks," he repeated.

"Indeed, sir." I spoke slowly and calmly. Hopefully, that would mollify him after Challenger's outburst.

"Ah, yes." Ungern settled back into his throne. "Well. I might require their help. I might not." He pointed to me. "You're Irish?"

He must have an ear for accents, however slight. "Yes, sir."

"Your countrymen, Yeats, wrote a poem about me—though he didn't know it." He cleared his throat. "What rough beast, its hour come at last, slouches toward Bethlehem to be born?" He rested pale fingers on his chest. "I am that beast. I am the Second Coming."

"Of what, exactly?" Reilly asked.

"Of the Khans, of course!" Ungern sounded exasperated, like he was explaining simple matters to a small child. "Genghis Kahn, Kublai Kahn, Tamerlane and his Golden Horde. They live on in me. It is way of Buddhism— of souls, reincarnated to live again. The souls of those great warriors live on in me, and I will honor them by raising a mighty host and sweeping across the world. Clearing away the Bolsheviks, the Jews, the decadents—any who stand against me." His voice boomed through the cave. Charlie and the other Neanderthals huddled together, terrified by this bellicose madman. "I am the punishment of God. If you had not committed great sins, God would not have sent a punishment like me upon you!"

After that, he paused for breath.

I had interviewed numerous egomaniacs in my time—I even counted Professor Challenger himself initially amongst their number—but this fellow took the cake. "So, what is your plan, then? Your battle plan?"

He raised his hands and pointed down the slope to the corral. "I was led here by destiny. I have tamed the mighty beasts. They shall accompany me to Mongolia, where I will take my place in the halls of Genghis Kahn. Then, once I make that fabled land my base, I shall strike west. The mammoths will carry my battle standard. The Bolsheviks will fall. Then the impertinent Poles will be crushed, and then I will reach the West. I shall succeed where my previous incarnations failed. I shall take the world, and transform the weaklings into a race of strong, pure warriors."

"What about those who don't wish to join into your grand plan?" Challenger asked. "Who have no intention of wearing furry hats and riding on the steppes?"

"I will have enemies. Of that I have no doubt." He bobbed his head. "I shall follow Genghis Kahn's example and put them to the test of the wagon wheel."

"I'm a little shaky on my Mongolian history, old boy. What's that?"

He put his hand about to his waist. "All men in conquered lands who are taller than the spoke of my wagon wheel shall be put to death. And I will make a mountain of their skulls."

Perhaps I am naïve considering the nature of the British Empire. The massacre of Amritsar, after all, was a result of British guns firing into a crowd of unarmed natives. And my own country currently faced the depredations of those criminals in uniform known as the Black and Tans, all under the command of His Majesty's Government. But I did not believe that England would ever support this madman, this would-be tyrant, and his bloodthirsty ways. Then again, if he had mammoths on his side, did he really need foreign help?

Esther finally spoke up. "You're a monster." She spoke to him in clear Russian. "A murderer. You kill because you enjoy it, and tell yourself a story to feel better. But you are just a monster."

He slapped her—a stinging blow to her cheek. She glared back, without even wincing.

Charlie rose to her defense with a keening cry. He brandished his spear and moved toward the Baron—only for the Cossack guard to reach him first. A rifle butt slammed into Charlie's back and dropped him to the ground, and boots pounded against his chest and face. He wailed and curled up.

"The local cavemen." Baron Ungern looked calmly at the beating. "They make excellent scouts and slaves. They'll serve me well in my conquests." Then his attention turned to Esther. "And who is this one? This woman who cannot keep a kind tongue in her mouth?"

If we told him the truth—that we had saved her from a group of refugees butchered by one of his patrols—he would probably end her life right there. And ours as well. I stared from Esther to Ungern. Challenger squared his large shoulders. Perhaps preparing to rush the baron.

Then, a call came from the field below. Ungern tore his eyes away from Esther and walked to the precipice. He peered down. "Ah yes." He raised his voice. "The prisoners." He motioned to the Cossacks behind him. "Bring one forth! Let us have a demonstration!"

Sure enough, the prisoners from the attack outside the Vyraj Valley now formed a ragged line in the center of the camp. The Soviets had been disarmed and huddled together. I caught a glimpse of Captain Nevskaya, her imperious nature vanished—now, as miserable as all her men. The Baron's men prodded them toward the center of the camp, a patch of snow marked with splotches of dried blood.

A low growl came from behind. The cave bear left its resting pace, pulled along on its chain by its Cossack handlers. They brought it down the trail and down to the place of the red snow, where a single, miserable Soviet conscript had been forced out as prey for the beast. The bear went willingly. It knew it was going to be fed.

Esther turned away. I did too. The screams and the roaring were terrible enough.

Afterwards, Baron Ungern raised his sword to the sky. "Tonight we feast!

I shall allow alcohol to be drunk—just for one night. We will celebrate our victory! Then, tomorrow, we leave Vyraj and travel to Mongolia. Our destiny awaits!"

His men cheered. The mammoths trumpeted.

I glanced at Sidney Reilly. He had stayed mostly silent during this entire exchange, but now he looked terrified. This was too much even for him.

That night, Baron Ungern's motley army did indeed throw a wild and raucous party. Evidently, he forced them to follow a sort of ascetic lifestyle, and allowed them to break the rules only occasionally. Now, they swilled vodka, sang their songs, and danced across the snow and around the fires. Neanderthal slaves brought them fresh bottles, which they swilled or hurled into the fire to create flashing explosions. The ice, shadow, and firelight transformed the world into a mad, reeling carnival, akin to a celebration of the demons in Hell.

I stood on a little hillock near the edge of the camp, my hands in my pockets, watching everything. After that fearsome display, I needed a moment of solitude.

For this place might be full of monstrous beasts, but there was no war—nothing like what had struck the world so recently. In that regard, the Vyraj Valley had been a heaven. Then, modern man had come in the form of Baron Roman Von Ungern-Sternberg, and turned it into Hell.

Esther joined me. Her eyes blazed. She stood next to me and we looked over the camp. "We have to stop him." She spoke clearly, with only a trace of fear. "What he did to my family, he will do to the world. He must be stopped." She grabbed a stick, poking out from the snow, and began drawing. Etching out the tents, the mammoth paddock, and the mountain. Making battle plans. "There—the armory." She etched out a bullet. "And here, the Bolshevik prisoners. We free them. Give them guns. Then, they'll destroy Ungern."

I shook my head. "Miss Esther, you have a noble soul—but we're just two people against an army."

She pointed. "Four."

Professor Challenger and Reilly walked back over the snow and joined us. "I made a little study of their encampment," Challenger explained. "I see you have as well."

"Esther wants to attack them." I shook my head. "She suggests stealing firearms from the armory, rescuing Captain Nevskaya and the Soviet prisoners, and leading an insurrection. It's madness—"

"Absolutely," Reilly agreed. He spoke in Yiddish to Esther—I couldn't make out much, but it sounded calm and well-reasoned.

Esther responded with what seemed like an insult.

Challenger sighed. "These fellows are right, Esther. An attack on the baron would be doomed to failure—"

"Thank you, professor—" I started.

"Unless it was planned well." He continued, ignoring me. "Your thinking is wise, Esther, but we need a distraction—and an escape." Challenger knelt by the map. "Look, here. The mammoth corral. I'll set the beasts free, and swipe one for ourselves." His eyes gleamed. "I studied from a mahout in India during my time on the Subcontinent."

"You're full of surprises," I said.

"Here's another: I've studied the use of demolitions. Perfect for clearing away all the stone that hides precious fossils. So I'll make a detour to their armory tent here, before I get the mammoths." He pointed to me and Esther. "What you have to do is get those Bolshevik prisoners. Set them free, convince them to join us, and I'll bring the ammunition. Making common cause with a pack of bloodthirsty revolutionaries irks me deeply, but needs must." His eyes settled on Reilly, all the joviality gone and replaced by a colder rage than I had seen before. "What are your thoughts, Mr. Reilly?"

"It's pure foolishness." Reilly shook his head. "We have to remain here. Gather what information we can, and then report to British Intelligence and—"

"I rather thought you might say that." Challenger approached him. "And I'm sorry. But once again, needs must."

His fist shot out—an out-of-nowhere right hook that put all his strength to use. The professor struck Reilly right in the head, and even over the wind and the songs of the celebrating Cossacks, the crack of the blow echoed. Reilly's eyes popped open and his tongue lolled. He dropped senseless in the snow.

Challenger shook out his fingers and winced. "He might've turned traitor. We can't risk it."

Esther looked at him. "Then, you'll go? To get the mammoths?"

"And leave Mr. Malone to the prisoners," Challenger agreed. "I'd normally insist that you stayed put—too dangerous for a woman your age—but I feel it would be a waste of breath." He offered his hand. "Best of luck to the both of you."

We shook his hand and headed out.

My heart pounded as Esther led me through the camp, past the rows of tents. She had scouted it out and knew where to go. I had faced death a thousand times in Professor Challenger's company, but somehow, this was worse. For we

"Esther wants to attack them."

weren't going up against some natural phenomena or hungry beast, but men—men with a seemingly infinite capacity for cruelty. If Baron Ungern caught us, a quick death would be the best we could hope for, and I sincerely believed we wouldn't even get that.

We reached a large tent at the end of the row, facing the snowy fields. A plump Cossack in a stained robe sat on a chair by the entrance, drool in his Father Christmas-sized beard as he snoozed. Esther put a finger to her lips. I went still as she leaned down and took the ring of keys from his belt. Then she held open the tent flap and we went inside.

The Bolsheviks—about a score of them—sat in a ragged circle with chains on their arms and legs, all connected to the tent post. They shivered in their ragged uniforms. Captain Nevskaya perked up. "The English spy. The Jew girl." She cocked her head. "What are you doing here?"

"We've come as your liberators," I said, as Esther undid the lock at the center. The chains fell down and she passed the key to the nearest soldier. "My friend the professor intends to move against the baron. It would be mighty decent of you to lend a hand."

Nevskaya stared at us, even as the chains rattled to the ground. "Fight alongside imperialist dogs like you? I think not."

"Then you'll die here." Esther glared at her. "Challenger will be here soon. Prepare yourself."

Now, the Soviet commander came to her feet. "You think I'll take orders from you?" She glared down at Esther. "Shtetl trash, who couldn't even—"

The tent flap opened. The Cossack emerged, covering us all with a shotgun. "Eh?" He swayed drunkenly, but that shotgun could wipe us all out. "What are you doing?" Vodka stunk on his breath. "You shouldn't be standing. Sit down. All of you."

Would our plan end so soon? A simple case of Nevskaya making too much noise and waking the guard. Pure rotten luck. I raised my hands and stepped closer to the shotgun, my heartbeat now loud as thunder. "Sir?" I tried to speak calmly. "Sir, I urge you to—"

"The handsome Englishman. I make you less handsome now..." He reached for the trigger.

Then gasped and staggered. A reddened spear point, slick with his gore, burst forth from his open mouth. The Cossack shuddered once, dropped his shotgun and fell to the ground.

Charlie Chaplin, our Neanderthal friend, tugged out the spear. He stood outside, along with a score of other Neanderthal warriors—all armed. His eyes went right to Esther, and he offered his arms. "Esther—you hurt?"

"Not at all." She walked closer to him and took his hand. "Thanks to you."

A huge, dark shape approached, emerging from the mist to stand next to the tent. I walked out of the tent, followed by Captain Nevskaya and her men. We stood amongst the Neanderthals as a mammoth trotted its way down through the ranks of the tents. Frost rose with every heavy footfall, and its great trunk swayed down. Professor Challenger sat on the mammoth's neck, in the position of mahout.

He gave us a wave. "Found some friends." He motioned to Charlie. "They were eager to join in. And I see you made some as well." The professor twisted around and pushed a wooden crate down from the howdah. It fell to the snowy earth with a rattle. "I brought them a wee present. Now, would you kindly climb aboard? We don't have much time."

Nevskaya went to the crate and pushed open the lid. Rifles waited in neat racks, along with bandoliers of ammunition. She shouted an order and her men commenced arming themselves. "We'll follow. Steal what horses we can."

"What happened to not fighting alongside imperialist dogs?" I went to the rope ladder, dangling down from the mammoth's side, and started climbing. Esther followed.

"Lenin would understand." Nevskaya slid bullets into the breach of her rifle. "What's your plan, professor?"

"Lead them out in the chaos. Seal the stones behind them. Lose them in the forest and make it to safety." Challenger reached back and helped me onto the perch of the howdah. More weapons waited, along with a crate containing dynamite and other explosive gear. "Stop anyone from reaching the Vyraj Valley again."

"What chaos?" Captain Nevskaya inquired.

The professor drew out the watch from his waistcoat, the silver chain shining in the light. "It should begin presently."

It did—an explosion shattering the Cossack bacchanalia. The first came from the west, an impossibly loud burst of rolling thunder accompanied by a brilliant cloud of fire. It swept up, erupting into the heavens and spitting a mass of snow, smoke, and fragments into the sky. That had to be the armory. Amazing with a stick of dynamite, set amidst other explosives and ammunition, could do.

Another explosion roared to life a moment later, this one from the other end of the camp. Mammoth trumpets followed. I peered through the tents, smoke, and chaos. The mammoths were free, and in their panic, charged right out of the corral and into the ranks of Baron Ungern's army. Their shaggy forms charged everywhere, trumpeting in panic as their heavy feet, tusks, and trunks went into deadly use against their former masters.

Baron Ungern's men shouted out panic and ran about, going for their weapons as they struggled to figure out what was happening. A squad of Cossacks hurried toward us from around a row of tents, screeching out a warning as they attempted to rise their rifles. Neanderthal spears and arrows met them, and a charging mammoth wiped out the rest. It sent one Cossack spiraling into the air with a flick of its truck, and crushed the others under its feet.

I cast a glimpse at Professor Challenger, the author of all this destruction. He was smiling, a naughty schoolboy who has disrupted his teacher's class with a particularly delicious prank.

"Let's ride back to the pass." He patted the mammoth's head. "Come along, then."

And we were off.

Our flight through Vyraj Valley seems to me like a half-remembered nightmare. We pounded through the camp, Challenger pausing every few moments to fire his carbine at some massed Cossacks—gaining their attention. Though, with Captain Nevskaya's Bolshevik soldiers close behind, that was hardly necessary. They raided the stables, and soon we had an accompaniment of cavalrymen, who rode around the mammoth and exchanged fire with the baron's men on our way out of the camp. Tents burned, mammoths trumpeted and trampled, and the Neanderthals pitted their spears and clubs against guns and sabers.

Then, we had left the camp behind and rode across the open plains—with everything Baron Ungern had in hot pursuit. A look over my shoulder showed them, following after us in a wild column. A great mass of horsemen, Baron Ungern's collection of killers from across the continent, all with their horses at a gallop and their swords raised high. Their wagons bearing machine guns followed us. There, riding at their head on a pure white stallion, came the Baron himself. His cloak billowed behind him, and he held up his sword, pointing the bejeweled weapon in our direction.

The chaos caused by the explosions and the mammoth stampede had bought us time. We would reach the pass, place the charges, and lure them out of Vyraj Valley and lose them in the woods before they could catch up to us.

Or at least, that was what I hoped.

At least we had a friend. Charlie gripped the rope ladder from the mammoth's side, his spear held in one hand as he dangled over the snow. "Easy, my friend!" Esther reached down and gripped his hand. "We'll make it through."

Challenger pointed. "Ah, in fact—here we are. The pass itself. Get that dynamite ready, would you, my boy?"

I fumbled with the crate behind us. Balance on the mammoth's moving back proved nearly impossible. Somehow, I took out one bundle of dynamite and a good amount of fuses without managing to fall off. I looked back up and stared ahead. The sunlight glinted on something metal, set on the rocks.

A machine gun, placed on a bipod and facing us.

"Reilly." Challenger slowed the mammoth. The Soviet horsemen around us went from a gallop to a canter. Our strange party reached the entrance of the pass. Sure enough, there was Sidney Reilly, perched on an outcropping covering the pass—the machine gun aimed straight at the howdah. He must have stolen it, and a horse, from Baron Ungern's encampment in the chaos, and made his way here.

Now, he had a winning hand.

"What do you intend to do with that machine gun, Mr. Reilly?" Challenger asked. Below us, Captain Nevsakaya's men went to a trot. They still had their rifles, but the machine gun could wipe them and their horses away in an instant.

Reilly crouched behind the trigger of the beastly weapon. "I have yet to decide. If I cut you down, Baron Ungern will doubtlessly reward me. Maybe make me one of his chief lieutenants. I could do with friendship to the heir to Genghis Kahn, couldn't I?"

"He's a monster!" I called. "A madman!"

"I have aligned myself with tyrants since I became an informer for the Okhrana. Since I started working for your government." His face had gone red below his bowler. Was it shame? Could someone like Reilly really feel that? "That's how I survive. I worry about myself and my fortunes and I get to live. That's my bargain." His eyes went to Esther. She just glared at him, her eyes fierce. "What? What do you have to say? What have you ever done, but huddle in the snow and die to the blades of attackers?"

She whispered something. A lilting song—a little prayer. Spoken in Hebrew.

"You don't get to do that to me!" Reilly gripped the triggers. "You think I feel guilt? Compassion? That there's any of that for me to feel? I tell you, girl, there is nothing!"

She continued singing her prayer. And Reilly had to recognize it.

Reilly shouted back—and his refined Russian vanished. Replaced with Yiddish. The same language Esther spoke. "I've left it behind. I've killed it! It is dead."

"But look around you, *landsman*," Esther replied. "We are in the Valley of the Dead."

His mouth opened. He closed his eyes for a long time and his lips moved, mouthing her words. Then, he reached over and racked the machine gun. "Cover your ears."

The machine gun roared, firing past us—and at the Cossack cavalry behind us. Even though I covered my ears, the shots were deafening. Reilly peppered them with a number of long, terrible bursts. When it was over, he reached for another belt and threaded it into place.

He had made his decision after all.

Challenger grinned. "Well done, Reilly, my boy! Keep up the fire. I'll do what I can."

He grabbed the dynamite from me and leapt down, scrambling toward the mountain pass with an almost boyish vigor. He went to work immediately, placing the dynamite candles amongst the stones and connecting them with wire. The assorted blasting caps and charges seemed like arcane instruments to me, but Challenger worked them with aplomb.

Nevskaya gripped the reins of her horse. "Professor?" She pointed behind us. "They're gaining on us."

Another burst from Reilly. "And I'm running out of ammunition."

"Blast." Challenger looked up from his work, a bundle of wire connected to a plunger. "Well, that rather complicates matters, doesn't it?"

"What do you mean?" I asked.

"I thought I had enough time to get safely across the pass before detonating, but it appears that's not the case." His eyes blazed. "Someone must stay behind to push down the plunger. They'll have to wait, until the Baron's bastards leave the pass after the rest of us, and trigger the explosion. And that means—"

"They'll be trapped here."

"Maybe not forever. We can arrange an airship to come by. A rescue expedition. But for the time being, yes—they'll be trapped." He wiped his brow. "Malone, you must remember me to my wife and daughter. Tell them I'll see them again. Promise them—"

"You can't—professor, you can't—" But I knew he had made his decision, in an instant. He would take up the sacrifice, for despite all his bluster, he had a hero's heart.

"No." Esther interrupted. She descended from the ladder and crossed the snow. I watched her from the howdah, as she approached Professor Challenger with her head held high. "I'll stay." She held out her hand. Charlie strode over to stand next to her. "It is right. I have nothing left outside. But this one..." She put her arm around Charlie's broad shoulders. "He is like a king. A kind man. I have seen civilization and its cruelty. I wish for something else."

"You'll be his queen. A Queen Esther," I mused.

"Why not?" Esther asked.

"We had better hurry!" Reilly picked up the machine gun, cradling the weapon awkwardly in his arms. "They'll be on us soon."

Baron Ungern's cavalry column came rushing down the field now, all drawing their swords as one to match their leader's raised saber.

Challenger pressed the plunger into Esther's hands. "Go there, behind that rock. Wait until they pass—we want all of them locked out. And see if you can get the rear in the blast." He shook his hand. "We'll bring you back, brave girl. If you want."

She embraced him, before clutching the detonator and hurrying away.

"Professor!" Nevskaya shouted. "Now?"

"Now." He pulled himself back up the rope ladder, grunting with exertion before settling on the mammoth's neck. A pat on the head and twist of the legs and the mammoth started off again. Back through the pass—back to the living world.

Reilly dropped down and landed next to me. He extended the tripod, aiming the machine gun behind me. I helped him as best he could. It chattered to life again as the mammoth broke into a run, and with the Bolshevik horsemen galloping alongside us, we rocketed through the pass. Each step sent a jolt through my bones, and the machine gun thundered next to me and spat out lead at our pursuers.

They reached the pass a moment later. Battle cries and bullets flew in our direction. I gripped the edge of the howdah and tried to hold on. Challenger was laughing, bellowing out his delight as we rode on, the wind tearing at us.

Through that valley, and out to the Leshy's Rest.

Baron Ungern's men swarmed in after—and that's when Esther did her job. The explosion ripped to life, the bundles of dynamite on both sides of the rock wall filling the pass with fire, dust, and chunks of stone and ice. The blast sent me tumbling back, nearly out of the howdah. Reilly grabbed my leg, and I looked back as stone came crushing down—burying Cossacks and their horses and locking away Vyraj Valley forever.

Then we were out, running amongst the trees. The mammoth trumpeted—almost triumphantly. I sat up. Nevskaya shouted with a savage glee as well, and Challenger let out a deep, enthusiastic belly-laugh.

We had brought war to this ancient land and won.

Until the baron's voice came from the dust. "Challenger!" He emerged, saber in one hand and pistol in the other. "I will have your head yet!" He took aim.

Except that he never got to fire. A tawny blur came at him from the side. Shining claws, feline agility in a powerful pounce, and great saber jaws flashed down onto the robed Baron Roman Von Ungern-Sternberg. He spun about, going for his saber as the saber-tooth tiger brought him down to the earth.

Snow and dust consumed them all. I did not know which of those monsters succeeded.

We bid our farewells to Sidney Reilly at the same disreputable alehouse in Vladivostok—now firmly under the control of the Bolsheviks. It was only thanks to Captain Nevskaya, who had given us passes and promised us firing squads if we returned that we could leave Russia at all.

A steamer would take the professor and I to Yokohama and then to England—and the mammoth would not be joining us. We had bid it farewell somewhere in the woods, perhaps to find a way back to the Vyraj Valley its home, just as Challenger and I would.

Now, we clinked a set of vodka glasses and drank deeply. The acrid liquid still burned my throat and made me gasp, much to the amusement of my drinking partners. "Hah! You've still got a lot to learn, my boy." Challenger refilled. "And what about you, Mr. Reilly? Can I not implore you to join us on the steamer?"

"Too much work to be done, for King and Country." He shrugged.

"And the danger?" I wondered.

"I'll accept it. The lying, the dealing, the spying—this is where I must practice my trade." He hoisted up his tumbler and stared at the clear liquid. "I am like those beasts in the Vyraj Valley. I belong nowhere else, until I go extinct." He sighed. "Let us drink to something happier. To Queen Esther, and her Neanderthal Kingdom." A smile appeared on his face—the first I had ever seen. "And to a magical place war will never again touch."

We clinked our glasses and drank to that.

The End

What Rough Beast Explanation

When it comes to Sir Arthur Conan Doyle, Sherlock Holmes is probably the number one creation, but The Lost World is a close second. I remember reading through the story some time in fifth grade, probably a little after I'd gone through my fully fledged Dino Kid phase, but when I was beginning to truly appreciate adventure literature for the first time. I've got fond memories of watching 2001 BBC adaptation with my sister, and the appreciating the dino action (and the Sir Arthur Conan Doyle cameo at the beginning!) of the 1925 version. So when Ron Fortier suggested a Professor Challenger story for an upcoming anthology, my love of prehistoric creatures and Lost World adventure led me to instantly agree.

I had a few ideas buzzing around, of ways to mash-up the prehistoric and the historic, but two suggestions in the submission guidelines really caught my eye: a war story and a lost world story. A Lost World story set during World War One—pterodactyls in the trenches!—had appeal, but the Great War felt like the most obvious setting. Instead, I settled a less well-known but still incredibly violent and world-shaking war with its roots in World War One: the Russian Revolution and Civil War.

That conflict has always fascinated me for its sheer complexity. Besides the simple Red Bolsheviks and White Tsarist Russians, you had a host of other factions, splinter groups, and warlords fighting for supremacy, to say nothing of the international response that sent soldiers from a dozen nations, including the US, into Russia. One figure in particular stands out for sheer evil: the mystical warlord Baron Roman Von Ungern-Sternberg. A psychotic war criminal, obsessed with Eastern Mysticism, who eventually took over Mongolia, he might be as close to a real-life pulp villain as you can find. The book The Bloody White Baron by James Palmer has all the information needed about this infamous figure.

I decided to combine his story with a type of Lost World that Challenger hadn't already visited—one with prehistoric mammoths, saber-tooth tigers, and Neanderthals instead of dinosaurs and Ape Men. Those creatures have the same sort of fantastic appeal as dinosaurs, and actually shared the earth (and devoured) our ancestors as well. But I needed another character, one to serve as a guide to Challenger and Malone through the chaos. I instantly knew another historic figure who would work: Sidney Reilly, a Russian-born, possibly

Jewish Tsarist Secret Police double-agent who became a British superspy and possible inspiration for James Bond before he met his end to the Bolsheviks in 1925. Showcasing his story, along with some of the real war crimes that Baron Ungern unleashed on the Jewish people during his pogroms, felt like it led to an interesting contrast: the savagery of modern times compared to the relative peace of the Lost World. And because I didn't want the only Jews in the story to be victims or rogues like Reilly, I came up with the idea of Esther, who ends up saving the day and becoming a Queen of the Neanderthals.

The result is a story I loved writing and I hope you enjoyed reading as well.

MICHAEL PANUSH is a lifelong writer and Sacramento native.

His books with Curiosity Quills include The Stein and Candle Detective Agency, featuring a pair of occult detectives in the 1950s, Dinosaur Jazz, a story about a Lost World battling against the forces of modernization; The El Mosaico series, an occult Western about a Frankenstein bounty hunter. With Pro Se Press, he created Ape's Honor, an alternate history adventure of a noble gentleman gorilla in a world of talking animals. With Airship 27, he created The Dagger Men, a Novel of the Clay Shamus—a story of a golem detective, and The Dead Sheriff, Volume 5: A Cold and Lonesome Grave, a novel about the undead Western avenger created by Mark Justice. His short fiction has been published in Towers of Metropolis, George Chance: The Green Ghost, Pulp Mythology, Volume Two, and Bass Reeves, Frontier Marshal, Volume 5. His most recent work for Airship 27, The Stone-Law: Blood-Spiller's Quarry, a prehistoric crime novel starring a neanderthal detective, is out now.

His new novel, Nathan the Rat, A Tale of the Dark Forest, is a medieval woodland fantasy about an orphan rat in a world at war.

He lives and teaches in Sacramento.

Follow him on the web at michaelpanush.com and on twitter at https:// twitter.com/Michael_Panush

The Unseen Star
By Samantha Lienhard

I've decided to record the recent events that occurred on the island of Danuk, in case at some point in the distant future, it becomes necessary once again to understand the truth of the unseen star. At Professor Challenger's request, I will omit certain details that could prove catastrophic in the wrong hands, but everything else is recorded exactly as it occurred.

The whole strange incident began when I received a vague letter from Professor Summerlee asking me to call on him at my earliest convenience about an urgent matter. It had been some years since I last worked with Summerlee, and the aging professor's health was a concern in the back of my mind, so I wasted no time in heading to his home.

I arrived at nearly the exact same time as another old friend, and as we reached the door together, Lord John Roxton broke out into laughter. "I say, young fellah, this is too much to be a coincidence. I suppose old Summerlee called you up here too—what?"

"He did," I said. "Did your letter give you any indication of what this is all about?"

"Not a whit, only that he should like my help."

"It must be something important," I said. "I can't imagine him sending such a letter about a trivial matter."

"After you, then. I daresay he'll be pleased we arrived together."

Without further delay, we headed on in.

Now despite my concerns about Summerlee's age, by no means do I intend to imply that he lost any of his vigor. He greeted us at the door, his gaze afire with righteous indignation.

"Good, you're here," he said, without any of the pleasantries one might expect from an old friend. "Perhaps the two of you can knock some sense into that idiot acquaintance of ours, as he certainly had no interest in listening to me!"

Lord John and I exchanged glances. His light blue eyes glimmered with amusement. "What 'idiot acquaintance' would that be?"

"Professor Challenger!"

I stifled a laugh. So the professor had once again gotten Summerlee riled up, this time to the point where he called upon us for help. Curiosity rose up in me as I reflected on our past experiences with Challenger. Had he uncovered another seemingly-impossible truth at odds with Summerlee's rigid views of science?

"What has he done?" I asked.

"That idiot," Summerlee said, his thin beard wagging with each enraged word he spoke, "he's gone and joined a cult!"

This time I wasn't able to suppress my laughter.

"I'm serious." Summerlee fixed the two of us with a glare, no trace of humor in his expression or demeanor. "His recent behavior has been entirely irrational—even by the dubious standards he's set in the past."

"You actually mean he's joined a cult?" I asked. "An actual cult?"

"That doesn't sound like him at all," Lord John said. "I say, are you sure you've got that right?"

Indeed, I could scarcely wrap my mind around the idea of Challenger doing something so peculiarly out-of-character. While prone to fits of emotion and excited outbursts, he was an intelligent man who always reasoned his way through a situation before acting. He was not the sort of man to be duped by charlatans, nor the sort to subscribe to a new system of beliefs without the science to back it up.

"When the rumors of his... *peculiar* actions surfaced, I couldn't believe it myself," Summerlee said. "So I paid him a visit at The Briars to get to the bottom of it, and the moment I broached the issue, he shouted at me to mind my own business and threw me out!"

"Now that *does* sound like him," Lord John said with a chuckle.

Summerlee did not look the slightest bit amused. "I'm at a loss for what to do. As infuriating as that man can be, this is concerning. I'd hoped you two might talk to him. He especially views you fondly, Malone, so you might make progress where I failed."

I shrugged. "Under the circumstances, we can hardly ignore this. I'll pay Professor Challenger a visit and see what he has to say."

"I'll join you," Lord John said. "Who knows what we might find ourselves caught up in this time?"

Indeed, I could see his thoughts were running along the same path as mine. With such behavior being so grossly out-of-character for Professor Challenger, Summerlee's report might indicate something much deeper at work. I'm certain the allure of excitement called to Lord John just as much as his friendship with Challenger, and as for me, I felt it was important to learn the truth.

For if my time with Professor Challenger had taught me anything, it was that when he spoke, other men should take heed.

The next day, we set out for Challenger's home at The Briars. I'd spent the evening at the Savage Club searching for any gossip and rumors about the professor, an effort which rewarded me with the same tales that must have driven Summerlee to call upon him. Over the past few months, Challenger had been spotted in several clandestine meetings with unknown persons who wore hooded black robes, and one witness claimed to have seen a man matching the professor's build clad in a similar robe himself.

When I relayed this back to Lord John, he let out a low whistle. "I don't suppose you think it's true. It would be a nasty shock to get out there and learn the old chap has gone over the edge—what?"

"It's impolite to even entertain such a notion about a friend," I said sharply. "After all we've gone through alongside Professor Challenger, how can you even suggest it?"

Lord John lifted his hands with a laugh. "Settle down, young fellah, I mean no harm. Still, what do you think is going on?"

"Perhaps," I said slowly, as I put together the scattered theories I'd had ever since our meeting with Summerlee the day before, "this is all part of some plan. The professor rarely does anything without a reason. I think—no, I'm sure—he knows exactly what he's doing, and even his treatment of Professor Summerlee must have had a cause. Whatever lies behind his actions, it will make sense once all is revealed."

My companion clapped his hands together. "Well said, well said! It's no stranger than some of our other experiences—what?"

Indeed, this was how it was with most public incidents regarding Professor Challenger. Aggressive and blunt, his manner often drove people to dismiss him as a blustering blowhard, particularly when he presented one of his more outlandish discoveries. Yet he had been proven correct time after time, and I myself had long since stopped underestimating him.

When we reached the house, Austin answered the door and let us in, as taciturn as ever. Mrs. Challenger was there to greet us as well, and she welcomed us inside with a smile.

"It's good to see both of you," she said. "We get visitors so rarely these days."

Their behavior allayed any lingering concerns I might have had. For if there had been a dire change in Professor Challenger, his wife would surely be troubled by it and Austin would at least hint at some perturbation.

"My husband is in his study at the moment," Mrs. Challenger said.

After thanking her, we walked up the familiar steps to the second floor and made our way to the large study. The door was closed, and I knocked once before easing it open.

Open books and yellowed documents covered every bit of the mahogany desk, with diagrams and scribbled notes in the margins. Even more books covered the floor in untidy piles, some askew as if cast aside in a fury.

Behind the desk, a large telescope sat pointing up at the sky through the bow window, and peering through it stood Professor Challenger himself.

He turned to face us as we entered, and upon seeing us, his broad face split into a delighted smile that one could not help but return. He let out a hearty laugh. "Wonderful, wonderful! I knew it wouldn't be long before Summerlee sent the two of you my way."

Lord John's mouth opened, and he stepped forward with a huff of disbelief. "I say, do you mean to tell us you riled poor Summerlee just to get us here?"

"That was part of the reason, yes," Challenger said, his voice calm and even.

Although I'd expected to learn he had a plan, this raised more questions. "Is there a reason you couldn't simply write and ask us to come?"

The mirth faded from Challenger's face, and he beckoned me forward with one large hand. "Do look out the window, young Malone, and tell me what you see."

Puzzled, I joined him at the bow window and looked out over the grand view he had from this height. Yet nothing appeared out of the ordinary; the plain was as peaceful as ever, the distant golf course appeared to be operating as usual, and the woods to the south were quiet with no disturbance aside from a young couple out for a stroll.

"Everything looks normal to me," I said.

Challenger let out a heavy sigh. "Malone, I've come to see you as a good degree better than the usual rabble I deal with, but even you can't entirely avoid the pitfalls so common to your profession. If you would, kindly erase whatever half-baked notions you came here with and try to grasp the actual question I posed."

His rebuke puzzled me, but when I considered it, I realized he'd merely told me to state what I saw, not whether or not I'd seen anything unusual. "The surrounding land looks the same as it always does. There are men playing golf over at Crowborough and a couple walking along the edge of the woods."

"Aha!" Challenger's sudden exclamation startled me. "And what would you say that couple is out there for?"

I watched as the distant pair stopped to point at something up in the trees, after which the man produced binoculars and scanned the sky. "Birdwatching, if I had to guess."

"So one might assume," Challenger said. "Yet due to the timing of their arrival, a pattern of similar occurrences, and the particular areas of their focus, I can say with certainty that they are, in fact, watching this house."

I turned from the bow window to stare at the professor's humorless expression, while Lord John appeared similarly perturbed by Challenger's revelation.

"Any friendly overtures toward my friends might draw suspicion," he continued. "Therefore, I relied on Summerlee's intervention to bring the two of you here as unwanted guests as far as any surveillance will be concerned."

"Who would be so concerned with your doings?" I asked.

"A group of men with whom I have recently become acquainted," Challenger said in reply.

Lord John frowned. "The cult Summerlee told us about? You mean there's a shred of truth in it after all?"

"More than a shred, and that is why we must proceed with such secrecy." Challenger walked to his desk and beckoned for us to join him.

A closer look revealed that the curious notes and diagrams on his desk related to the position of the stars and constellations, which undoubtedly explained the telescope. From the little I saw, I hazarded an initial guess that the professor was tracking something up in the heavens.

Challenger fixed us both with a serious stare. "Have either of you heard of an island known as Danuk?"

Something about the name tugged at the corner of my memories, and I frowned as I tried to place it.

"There was some sort of flap about that place last year," Lord John said after a moment. "Something about the natives not wanting to be bothered."

"Of course," I said, as the name clicked, "we covered the controversy for weeks. The people who live on that island are a hunter-gatherer society, and the scientific community wanted to go there and study their ways. The natives asked to be left alone to better preserve their traditions, and after a great deal of arguing, the decision was made to leave Danuk in isolation."

"Precisely," Challenger said.

"What of it?" Lord John asked. "I scarcely see how this has anything to do with us."

"It has everything to do with us—with *all* of us," Professor Challenger said, his tone so serious that I knew in an instant he didn't mean merely the three of us standing together in the study but the human race itself. "For what if I told you the island of Danuk is not home to a hunter-gatherer society at all, but to a group of learned men who have made it the site of their secret meetings?"

We stared at him in shock.

"But… surely someone would notice," I managed at last.

"They have *not* noticed," Challenger said, "and your own assumptions demonstrate exactly why. The supposed natives who spoke up about wanting to remain isolated are merely actors, brought to Danuk to keep up the pretense and exploit the public's sympathy, all in order to keep this organization's activities a secret."

"That's abominable," Lord John said with a hiss of disgust. "Such deception not only makes fools of us, but casts suspicion on all the people who truly do wish to be left alone!"

"Why would anyone do such a thing?" I asked.

"If anyone learned what this group was planning," Challenger said, "they would assuredly meet with resistance. As such, secrecy is vital. They cover their tracks and keep their organization shrouded in mystery. Fortunately, an undertaking such as theirs would be impossible if they were forced to rely on the average person's intellect, and therefore they are always eager to recruit one such as myself. In their desire to turn my mind toward their own purposes, they have accepted my claim that I share their goals."

So the professor had infiltrated this organization, hence the rumors about him and his ill treatment of Summerlee.

"But who *are* they?" Lord John asked, his voice filled with frustration.

"They have no name," the professor said. "They see no need for one. Either you are one of them, or you are not. Either you know, or you are ignorant. External identification, therefore, becomes irrelevant."

"Sounds like a load of rubbish if you ask me," Lord John said under his breath.

I was inclined to agree, yet the more pressing issue was that Challenger must have seen these men as a threat, or he would not have called us here. "What are they trying to do?" I asked.

"Now we're getting to the crux of the issue." Professor Challenger waved his hand at the array of documents and books on his desk. "What led me to uncovering the truth about this organization was learning about the same phenomenon that has fascinated them for generations—millennia, even. For time immemorial, certain beliefs have been passed down until they reached their current form as this group's nearly incomprehensible goal."

A shiver of anxiety ran through me at his grave words, and I took another look at the constellations he had seemingly been studying.

"I would get straight to the matter at hand," he said, "and yet first I must lay down the basic groundwork to be sure I have not underestimated your potential ignorance. Are you aware that constellations change over time?"

"Of course," I said, pleased my passing knowledge of the heavens should meet with his approval. "Stars move slowly, and so over a long enough period of time, gradual changes can be noticed by observers here on Earth."

"Excellent!" he said with a laugh. "Then I don't need to begin my explanation with the basics. Yet I daresay you are not aware that certain constellations have had new stars appear."

"You mean they've gotten brighter over time?" Lord John asked.

"That is certainly what they would have you believe."

"Hang on," I said, unable to withhold a protest, "if you're saying entirely new stars have appeared in the sky, this should be a well-known phenomenon. Surely astronomers would have noticed and conducted a study."

This had become a matter of personal interest to me over the past year, and it was with some bitterness that I repeated the same words that had been patiently said to me.

Professor Challenger nodded. "That is a point we must consider." He waved his hand at the books in front of him. "I would like to draw your attention to the constellation Perseus, named for the famous hero of the Greeks. It is a well-known constellation, and it has from time to time been associated with misfortune due to the presence of the so-called 'Demon Star,' Algol."

His dismissive snort assured me that the Demon Star was not what this meeting was about, although I admit I still was at a loss of what exactly we *were* here to discuss.

"Algol aside," he said, "there is an entirely different star within Perseus that we must take note of. The northeastern section of the constellation includes a cluster of stars believed to be roughly 1,000 light-years away. However, one of the stars in this cluster, a bright star clearly visible from Earth, was never seen until approximately 2,000 years ago."

"How in blazes do you know that?" Lord John asked.

Challenger tapped his fingers on one of the books that covered his desk, this one aged and crumbling. "Ancient texts from that era include references to this sudden new star in the sky. The people of the time believed it to be the result of a sacred ceremony their ancestors performed and a sign that their gods were listening to them. Based on the tradition that had been passed down through the ages—of which only fragmented texts survived, forcing us to rely on the records from their descendants—a god came down from the heavens 4,000 years ago and wiped out their enemies.

"Most scholars have explained this as a meteor impact, and indeed, they are on the right track. However, that ancient people believed that by worshipping this so-called 'god' in the ceremony prescribed by it, they would win the favor of the heavens and gain dominance over the Earth. They passed down the ceremony to their descendants, as well as a message: when a new star appeared in the sky, it was time for the ritual to begin anew. 2,000 years ago, observers saw the new star and revived the ancient ceremony.

"Now, this brings us to the matter of a more recent phenomenon that you, my young friend, have personal knowledge of—the claim that a new star appeared in the sky.'"

The reminder brought a flush to my face, for after all I'd done to distinguish myself at the Daily Gazette, my story some several months past about a new star in the sky had made us such a laughingstock that McArdle roundly criticized me for not doing my due diligence ahead of time, and my career nearly ground to a halt.

In truth, I had done the research to make a compelling story out of the inexplicable phenomenon, yet no sooner had the article appeared in the paper than astronomers and academics wrote to us in droves to explain that the star in question was *quite* well-known and had been for years, and it simply changed in brightness enough to make it more easily visible.

It was not an incident I enjoyed recounting, although I'd had no doubt Challenger and Lord John were both aware of it already.

"This demonstrates entirely what is wrong with the scientific community," Challenger said. "Fools who believe they know everything are content to accept reports that line up with their pre-established beliefs without ever digging deeper. For you were in the right, Malone. The star was not merely dim in the past, as you were told. It was not visible at all."

Astonished, I shook my head. "How is that possible? I was shown records documenting its existence!"

"Records can be forged, reports can be falsified, and even men of science can be bribed or intimidated into silence."

"You mean this same organization is responsible? But why go through all the trouble of covering up such a thing?"

"I told you that ancient people believed the appearance of the new star in the Perseus cluster was a sign of favor from the gods. This belief persisted throughout the years as various groups passed down their belief in an ancient god that slumbered far from Earth, awaiting the day it would be awoken. The ceremony came to be known as the Triad Awakening. Once the three dormant stars appeared in the sky, the distant god would stir."

If any other man had said it, I would have scoffed at the absurdity, yet my history with Challenger told me to trust his word, and I found myself listening with rapt attention to hear where this strange tale would lead.

"Yet they did not see it as a benevolent god," he said. "Recall, if you will, how this began. The arrival of the first 'god' destroyed their enemies. That is what they believed completing the Triad Awakening would achieve. They called this sleeping god the Destroyer, an entity that would purge the world of life and preserve only its chosen disciples."

It was not the first time we had faced the potential for cosmic destruction, but a chill ran through me all the same.

He waved his hand in a dismissive gesture. "That is superstitious nonsense, of course, but every myth has an origin. Those ancient people did not simply invent the Destroyer out of fancy. Whatever fell from the sky that day had a connection to something real, and it gave them both the means and method to signal it. I believe there truly is something out there—not a god, but an ancient piece of technology, a machine with such incredible destructive power, it could easily be mistaken for a god by a primitive society, and the three supposed 'stars' are in fact lights to indicate its activation."

"How could such a thing exist?" Lord John asked.

"Who can say?" Challenger shook his head. "The records have become too muddled over time to make true sense of them, not least because of that organization's activities. They supplanted the Destroyer's disciples and came to the same conclusion as I. Yet this organization is not merely an idle group of observers. Rather, these learned men have applied all of their knowledge toward enabling the Awakening."

"If they don't believe it's a god," I said, "why do they want to activate it?"

"For power, of course. They are currently led by a man named Weiss, and he believes whoever completes the Triad Awakening will be able to control the machine."

"And... will they?" I asked.

Challenger snorted. "Unlikely. Even so, do you believe anyone should control power capable of devastating the Earth?"

I considered that for a moment and then shook my head. I was beginning to understand why he was so concerned about this.

"Can they actually do it?" Lord John asked. "Are you saying this 'Triad Awakening' really works?"

"My research—particularly once my show of good will earned me access to the organization's notes—suggests as much," Challenger said. "Two 'stars' have appeared, with the third yet to come. Moreover, the number 2,000 appears to be important; the gap of 2,000 years between the appearance of the first star and the appearance of the second is not accidental."

"Hang on," Lord John said, "that's all very well and good to know, and I suppose we ought to leave notes to warn our descendants, but if what you're saying is true, the third star isn't set to appear for another 2,000 years."

"Correct," Professor Challenger said, "but we are the ones who must face this problem."

"I don't see how."

"Perhaps young Malone has some insight where you have failed."

I puzzled over the matter, for Lord John's assessment sounded valid—and then the issue struck me. "Why, it takes time for the light from those stars

"Two stars have appeared with the third to come."

to reach us! *Light-years*, the number of years it takes. By the time we see something in the heavens, it's already occurred long ago."

"Exactly," he said. "I'm pleased your wit was able to reach that point, even if it took some time before you grasped it."

"I'd have gotten there eventually," Lord John said under his breath, as if irked by the slight.

Challenger spread out one of the many sets of documents that lay on the table. "Allowing for variance due to the size of the construct itself, the two stars that heralded the start of the Triad Awakening are both approximately 1,000 light-years away from the Earth. We must assume the same is true of the third."

"So then if it becomes visible 2,000 years from now," I said, "that means it will actually be activated 1,000 years from now, because it takes 1,000 years to become visible from Earth."

"Correct—if it is awoken. It cannot activate on its own. This construct appears to have set intervals of time during which it can receive a signal. The ancient rituals used for the first two have developed into more sophisticated forms under the current organization's guidance, particularly since whatever means those civilizations had of sending their signal has been lost to the ages, but it still requires time."

His gaze burned into me, and I drew a sharp breath. "Radio signals! It would take the same amount of time for a radio signal to get out there, wouldn't it? Another 1,000 years."

"Precisely," he said.

Lord John shook his head. "By George, then we don't have much time! You're saying this is the year—what?"

Challenger nodded. "The numbers are estimates, but the appearance of the second star suggests the time is close. By the records passed down through the organization, Weiss and the others believe this year—yes, this very year—is the time to complete the Triad Awakening."

No wonder he had kept this quiet. Had he gone public with this knowledge, it would have been dismissed as the ravings of a madman.

"What can we do?" I asked.

"We need to disrupt their plans and ensure the Triad Awakening cannot be completed. For if the unseen star appears, it will surely mean doom for our descendants."

"You want us to stop the appearance of a star 1,000 light-years away," Lord John said, "and one we can't even see, at that? I do hope you have a plan, old chap."

"Stopping Weiss and his organization is key." Challenger fixed us both with a serious look. "However, these are dangerous men. If you join me in this venture, you'll both be at risk."

"We're hardly the sorts to shy away from danger," Lord John said with a grin, undoubtedly relishing the adventure this situation demanded.

"I agree," I said. "Have you ever known us to back down out of fear? I'm in."

Challenger nodded. "I'm pleased to see you've met my expectations again. Now, our greatest obstacle will also be our greatest advantage, and that is Weiss's paranoia. His obsession with secrecy means that although he has seen every recruit to the organization, including myself, the rest keep their identities a secret from one another. If you can infiltrate the island, I can get you into their base."

I rubbed my chin. "I suppose I could go there as a reporter. McArdle might be agreeable to a follow-up story on the natives of Danuk after what happened last year. Then when the time is right, I'll pull back the curtain to reveal the whole ugly picture."

The more I thought about it, the more it disturbed me beyond simply the dangers of their monstrous plan. They had played on public sympathies to present themselves as a primitive society that wanted to preserve its traditions. Whether or not we could stop them, we had to bring the truth to light—if only to show the world who was responsible.

"We'll say I'm working with you," Lord John said "A lone reporter heading into the wilderness could use protection—what?"

"Good," Challenger said. "Now, there is one more thing." He opened a drawer of his desk and pulled out a small, wrapped package, which he handed to me. "Take this with you and keep it safe. Do not let anyone take it from you."

"What is it?" I asked.

"If the worst comes to pass, it might be our salvation," he said gravely.

Although I didn't understand, I tucked the small box into the pocket of my coat.

"I'll leave it to you to arrange passage to Danuk," Challenger said. "I would have liked to arrange it, but such action might arouse suspicions."

A concern struck me then, and I walked to the bow window again. Indeed, the supposed birdwatchers were still out there. "Considering you used Professor Summerlee to call us here so you wouldn't be witnessed contacting us directly, won't they be suspicious if they see us leaving like old friends?"

Challenger clapped his massive hands together, a fiery glint in his eye. "That's solved easily enough. I'll just have to throw you out."

Before either of us could protest this plan, he had grabbed us by our shirt collars. With a ferocious bellow, Challenger ran us out of his study and down the stairs. He drove us past his startled-looking wife, threw open the door, and flung us out into the street.

As the door slammed shut, I dusted myself off and let out a sigh. That unceremonious dismissal would surely do the job for anyone watching.

"We're really in it this time, aren't we?" Lord John asked.

I looked up at the sky, where an invisible threat lurked almost an incomprehensible distance away. "I daresay you're right."

And so it was that we found ourselves preparing for an expedition to the island of Danuk.

A few days after obtaining permission to visit Danuk on behalf of the Daily Gazette, Lord John and I began our journey. We traveled first to the coast of Africa, from which we could charter a boat to take us the rest of the way. It was difficult to arrange transportation, both due to Danuk's unfriendliness toward visitors and the island's isolation; many past would-be explorers had died attempting to make the journey. However, we'd managed to find a boatman who swore he was capable of safely reaching Danuk's shores safely and was willing to return each morning to see if we were ready to go back.

One condition of our visit was that no weapons were allowed, much to Lord John's frustration when his rifle was refused. Nevertheless, he put on a smile and seemed almost pleased by the danger of heading into such a precarious situation unarmed. He lived for the thrill of adventure, after all, and I suspected that motivated him just as much as the importance of our mission. For my part, I was just relieved they took no notice of my small package from the professor.

Danuk was a fair distance from the coast, which increased its isolation. No doubt this was why the organization had chosen it, to better aid their deception.

It was a quiet journey, as neither of us had much to say.

When we reached the isolated island, we confirmed with the boatman that he would wait two hours in case we needed to leave immediately, then return each morning to wait one hour until we were ready to leave. Since we didn't know how long our business here would take and would have no way of contacting the mainland, it felt like the best plan.

With that confirmed, Lord John and I set out away from the beach. Almost immediately, the bushes up ahead parted and three men emerged.

They looked for all the world like what they were supposed to be—native islanders from an isolated culture.

One stepped forward and spoke to us in accented English. "No outsiders.

We made this clear."

I adopted a friendly smile and cleared my throat. "I'm from the Daily Gazette. Last year, we covered the controversy about Danuk, and now we'd like to do a follow-up story."

"No story. You are not wanted here."

We had prepared for this possibility, since we knew it was unlikely we'd be welcomed. "You misunderstand me," I said. "We have no wish to intrude on your lives. It's quite the opposite. The public has become interested in Danuk again, and there's a growing movement to overturn last year's decision."

His eyes narrowed. He said something to his companions in an unfamiliar, short-syllabled language. The second man's gaze darkened, and he muttered something under his breath in the same language. The other, who appeared to be the youngest of the three, looked away with a troubled expression.

"We want to help you," I said. "If we write a follow-up story about how peaceful life is on Danuk, it should be enough to convince people to leave you alone."

The translator returned his suspicious gaze to us. Sweat rolled down the back of my neck, but I continued to smile. We were in no true danger yet. If something happened to us here, it would bring far more attention to the island. The organization would wish to avoid harming us until we interfered with them directly.

At last, he nodded. "You will be honored guests for one week."

"That sounds fine," I said.

With any luck, we would have reunited with Challenger and completed our work long before then.

He and the two guards led us away from the beach, through thick foliage and towering trees into a small village. Men and women looked up at our approach, and the translator spoke to them with much gesturing in our direction.

It was a curious thing to see the village with the foreknowledge given to us by the professor. If we had truly come for the purpose I stated, the villagers' act would have surely fooled us—although perhaps Challenger himself would have seen through their deception with his keen eye for detail. Yet as much as it pains me to admit it, I would have accepted the village at face value and congratulated myself on getting such an excellent story.

Yet with what we knew, it took on a surreal quality. Small huts matched those I'd expect to see in a primitive village—almost too well, as if constructed by someone who knew what we thought we'd see. Religious iconography near one hut looked equally fitting, yet some of the symbols were inconsistent, as if picked arbitrarily instead of truly holding meaning. The entire village was built to show us what we wanted to see, a set designed to play on our assumptions of what such an isolated culture was like.

It felt insulting, both to us and to the actual societies their façade was set up in mimicry of. Something must have compelled the people here to go along with the organization's ploy, and as our guides gave us a brief tour, my gaze went again to the youngest guide, who appeared so troubled.

Whether they were paid or threatened into compliance, such an elaborate deception necessitated that whole families be brought to live in this fake civilization. Perhaps not all were fully on board.

At last, the translator led us to a small hut on the edge of the village. "You will stay here."

I shook my head. "That won't be necessary. We don't want to disturb your daily lives any more than we have already. We'll be able to take care of ourselves."

Lord John lifted the tents we'd brought for emphasis.

The translator's eyes narrowed slightly. "Our honored guests will stay *here*."

No amount of protesting would get him to change his mind. Our plan of pitching our tents some distance away and sneaking out in the night had already been dashed.

Once we were alone in the hut, Lord John met my gaze over the small amount of food that had been provided to us. "Quite the situation, isn't it, young fellah? What now?"

"We play our roles and wait for an opportunity to get away."

We kept our voices low, in case the guards outside the door understood English.

"Do you suppose the professor is already here?" he asked.

"No doubt, waiting for us to join him."

"I daresay we won't get out of here easily."

"Some of the villagers might be sympathetic," I said. "I don't suppose you recognize their language?"

To my dismay, Lord John shook his head. "It's not one I know."

"Right then," I said. "We have one week. Tomorrow, we'll see what we can do."

I slept well enough during the night, with the small package entrusted to me by the professor kept close at hand to ensure it was safe. The next morning, I left the hut. No one stopped me as I walked through the village, although curious gazes followed me. The moment I approached the border with the jungle, however, two guards stepped into my path.

One raised his voice in a sharp cry, and soon the translator emerged from a hut and hurried over to join us.

"You must stay in the village," he said. "Please understand."

"I'd like to see more of the island for my story," I said. "Are there other villages? Do you grow crops? What sort of animals do you hunt?"

"I will answer your questions," he said, "but you must stay here."

"Why?"

"The other villages have no contact with the outside world. You understand."

The last was not a question, and I was politely—but firmly—escorted away from the border. After a brief session where the translator gave me all sorts of good-sounding answers that I dutifully recorded for my story, I returned to our hut and reported my failure to Lord John.

"Maybe next time, young fellah," he said, with a sympathetic smile.

A few hours later, it was his turn. Lord John sauntered outside to join a group of young men gathered at the village entrance with bows and spears, and while I watched from the door, he introduced himself with a hearty handshake for their leader.

"Off for some hunting?" he asked. "I'm known to be a fair shot back home, and it would be entertaining to see the sort of game you have around here—what?"

The hunters didn't seem to quite know what to make of Lord John, but it wasn't long before the translator appeared and thwarted his efforts. My friend rejoined me in the hut with a huff of annoyance, but I could tell from the gleam in his eye that he'd far from given up.

Over the next three days, we played the content guests in the village. I continued to take notes on everything told to me, since all of these details would help explain how this façade was perpetrated once I had a chance to write my true story.

They had invented customs in the way a writer might develop a fictional culture for a story, and their daily lives preyed upon stereotypes and assumptions that we and our readers were assumed to have about the natives. A dance one night was intended to contact their ancestors; a hunting party set out with a young man to help him prove himself and step into adulthood. On and on it went, and through it all I kept an eye on the young man who appeared so disturbed the first day we arrived, whose name was Makalo according to the information Lord John gleaned through his repeated attempts to join the hunters.

Makalo and several of the others—mostly the younger men, and also some of the wives—appeared uncomfortable with the charade and responded more favorably to Lord John's overtures of friendship. Soon it was not uncommon to see him amongst the hunters, although the translator ensured he never actually left the village with them.

Since Makalo was frequently assigned to deal with us, I attempted to foster a sense of camaraderie with him as well. I met his gaze when our paths crossed, made sure to thank him whenever he brought our food, and waved when I saw him in the village.

But if his mood improved, Lord John's only darkened the longer we remained. I recalled that he despised any sort of exploitation and once spearheaded a slave uprising in South America, and if we didn't act soon, he might decide to drop subtlety and lead a revolt.

We needed to make our move.

Makalo arrived that morning with our meal. After setting the food down, he turned to make a hasty retreat as usual, but I reached out to stop him.

"Wait, Makalo."

He froze.

"We're not your enemies," I said, my voice hushed in case anyone might overhear. "We're not here to disrupt your lives."

His gaze contained no hint of comprehension, and I sighed. I'd hoped he might secretly understand English. If we couldn't communicate, this would become that much harder. He was clearly disturbed by the way things were going on Danuk, but I had no way of conveying our knowledge to him. Yet he still watched me, as if curious about what I was trying to say.

"We're looking for a group of Europeans. Men like us." I pointed to myself and Lord John. "We're looking for a man named Weiss."

His eyes widened.

He knew the name of the organization's leader, then.

Makalo said something in his own language, of which I understood nothing save for *Weiss*. His expression was troubled, his gaze dark.

Lord John cleared his throat. "We're here to stop Weiss." He added a hard edge to his tone and mimed a stabbing motion to illustrate his words. "Any chance you can help us out, young fellah?"

I pointed out in the direction that led deeper into the island. "We need to find Weiss."

Makalo looked at us for a long time. Then he gave a short nod and left.

"Well, that's that," Lord John said with a grin. "Either he's got a plan or he'll betray us. All we can do is wait to see which is which."

"I don't think he'll betray us," I said. "At least not if he understood. You saw his face when I mentioned Weiss."

"This Weiss chap must be a piece of work. Should be interesting when we reach him—what?"

"I just hope the professor is waiting for us," I said.

That evening, the festival began. With a small supply of food packed away, Lord John and I positioned ourselves near the edge of the assembled villagers in the hopes of finding an opportunity to leave despite the guards stationed around the borders and how much we stood out. A great bonfire blazed in the center of the village, and the festival began with several of the young women performing a dance around it.

Partway through the dance, Makalo drew near. He didn't say a word, but simply pointed at the hut.

I glanced at Lord John, who shrugged and opened the door. "What do you suppose he's up to?"

"I don't know, but we should find out soon."

We went inside.

It didn't take long. Shouts from the village rang out over the sound of the music, and I opened the door a crack to look out. Makalo stood at the far end of the village, pointing into the trees and shouting. The guards stationed near the entrance ran toward him, as did several others.

"That's our cue," I said.

We crept out of the hut. With everyone distracted by Makalo—if I had to guess from their reactions and demeanor, he'd pretended we already escaped in that direction—we darted to the unguarded boundary. I dashed into the thick foliage and glanced back.

Lord John was gone.

Momentary alarm made me pause, but he emerged a moment later with a large bow and a quiver of arrows in his hands.

"Saw the hunters stash this the other day," he said. "It's better than nothing."

I had some misgivings about whether or not his skill with rifles also extended to archery, not to mention our chances against a well-prepared organization with such a weapon, but as he said, some self-defense was better than none, and if anyone could do it, it was Lord John Roxton.

Chaos filled the village behind us, and I bid a silent salute to Makalo for his help before we raced away from our potential pursuers and disappeared into the jungle as the night deepened around us.

"Saw the hunters stash this the other day."

What followed was a night of tension and dread, as we crept through the jungle alert for any signs of pursuit. At one point, shouts echoed too close behind us for comfort, but we kept moving and soon lost the sounds in the distance.

The silence that descended became even more unnerving. We heard nothing as we moved through the trees, no rustling of animals, no chirping insects, nothing at all to suggest there was any wildlife on Danuk. There had to be living creatures here, since the villagers went hunting each day and even they couldn't perpetrate a deception to that degree. But whatever animals made this island their home, they had forsaken this section of the jungle entirely, and that cast an eerie tone over our expedition.

It was as if the island itself was telling us we weren't welcome. Go away, go away, go away, this imagined cry echoed through my mind with each step. My uneasiness only grew as we delved deeper into jungles that held none of the threats we faced on past expeditions, but rather some unseen force that implied a different sort of danger all together.

Then the tower came into view.

It extended almost to the treetops, hidden just enough so that it wouldn't be visible from the village or from planes flying overhead. The trees gave it natural camouflage, but as close as we were, it came to life as something out of place, a massive monolith sticking out from the natural foliage around it. Pure white stone formed its smooth walls, and they rose in a perfect column toward the sky, with no openings of any kind besides a single door at the front. At the top, a ring of telescopes visible through the tower's crenellations all pointed up toward the sky, and the effect put me in mind of tiny eyes staring toward that distant construct the organization pinned its mad ambitions on.

We stood there for a moment longer, and then Lord John grabbed my arm and dragged me further back, where we crouched concealed by the brush.

"What now?" he asked. In the unnatural silence, even his whisper sounded too loud. "It's all well and good that we made it this far, but I daresay we can't walk in through the front door."

"The professor must have a plan," I said. "He told us to come here, so I'm certain he planned ahead."

Lord John shook his head. "Then I suppose we've got to observe the tower—what?"

"For now," I said. "At the very least, surveying the situation should give us a better idea of what we're dealing with and what we should do from here."

We didn't dare set up an actual camp close to the tower, but we found a small clearing where we might rest comfortably while keeping watch for any sign of activity. The silence persisted, broken only by the occasional sound of distant pursuers, and so we took shifts during the night.

Nothing changed during our surveillance. When morning arrived, we ate some of the food we'd smuggled out of the village with us and continued to watch.

Footsteps through the brush made me freeze.

Lord John beckoned, and we crouched down under the thick leaves of the bushes around us to have as much cover as we could. Soon, a lone man emerged through the jungle from the direction of the village. As he drew closer, I recognized him as our translator. He walked straight to the tower.

Once there, he knocked in a curiously deliberate way, two quick knocks, then a pause, then a single knock, followed by another pause and then two more quick knocks.

The door opened, and a tall man stepped out.

A hooded black cloak completely shrouded his frame, and beneath the shadows of the hood, a white mask covered his face. A shiver of trepidation coursed through me. Surely this was Weiss, their leader. He was not a large man, but he carried himself with an almost regal bearing. This was not the sort of man used to being defied, and I almost pitied the translator for being the one to bring news of our escape.

"Why are you here?" he asked, his voice hard and cold, words clear despite a heavy European accent—German, if I had to guess.

"Those two men from the newspaper are missing," the translator said.

"What? How could you let this happen?"

"It happened during the night. They somehow slipped past our guards."

"Idiot!" Weiss struck the translator across the face with enough force to make him stagger back a step.

The translator lowered his head. "We won't make such a mistake again, sir."

"You may not have a *chance* to make another mistake. Those two men could ruin everything. No doubt they think they'll get the big inside story on Danuk's primitive tribe, and what will they find instead? They could stumble upon our entire operation! This is what I get for relying on someone like you to cover for us. All you had to do was put on your act whenever someone approached the island, but you couldn't even accomplish such a simple task!"

Although I remained tense, I inwardly breathed a sigh of relief. Our situation was precarious, but neither of them knew our true reason for being there. That meant Professor Challenger's cover should still be intact, and presumably Makalo's aid hadn't been discovered either.

"Find them," Weiss said in clipped tones. "Scour every inch of this island until you locate them and determine exactly what they have seen."

"And if they've seen…" The translator waved his hand at the tower.

"Then you will silence them. And it must appear to be an accident."

He nodded, not a trace of hesitation in his face.

Any doubts I might have had about Challenger's dire assessment of this organization were gone. Weiss wanted us dead if we'd seen the tower, and the translator was prepared to carry it out. Whatever they were up to, they needed to be stopped.

"Weiss!" a voice called from inside the tower.

My heart leaped. That was Professor Challenger's voice.

Weiss glared at the translator. "Don't disappoint us again." Then he whirled around and re-entered the tower. He said something, and although I couldn't make out the words, Challenger responded.

The door swung shut behind him with a resounding *thud*. The translator stared at the tower a moment longer, then turned and trudged away through the jungle. I let out a slow breath.

"He ought to know by now," Lord John said quietly.

I nodded. "Let's wait."

Three hours passed as we continued our silent surveillance, and then at last, movement caught my eye from the top of the tower. Amidst the ring of telescopes, someone walked toward the edge. A moment later, a rope dropped down over the side of the tower, long enough to nearly reach the ground and apparently tied to something at the top.

The figure on the tower, whom I assumed must be Challenger, turned away and vanished again.

Lord John laughed and shook his head. "Up for a bit of exercise, young fellah?"

"I suppose it's the only other way into the tower aside from the front door," I said, "and we can hardly go in that way. It'll be quite a climb, though."

"Should be a nice change of pace," he said. "A far cry better than sitting around waiting for the chaps from the village to find us—what?"

Since the tower had no windows, that would make it all the easier for us to climb up unseen. However, if anyone emerged from the tower while we were on our way up, they would spot us in an instant. We needed to hurry.

After a quick glance around to make sure we were alone, we hastened toward the tower. Up close, the walls were completely smooth, and I revised my initial impression to the perplexing possibility that the entire structure was carved from a single monolithic stone, hollowed out to form the tower, for there were no seams or masonry of any kind to justify its construction.

Fortunately, we were both well-suited to physical activity and dealt with similar exertions on past adventures. It was almost with a sense of nostalgia that I gripped the rope and began the difficult ascent.

It was slow going, and every moment I clung to the outside of the tower left me paranoid that someone would emerge from within and catch us. However, I pulled myself up hand over hand, until at last I crested the tower and clambered over the top.

The smooth white stone continued across the upper walls, disrupted only by a single wooden door that led inside. While I waited for Lord John to join me, I walked to the cluster of telescopes, all fixed upon a single point in the sky, and looked through them.

Despite it being daytime, a cluster of stars was visible through the lens. From my own knowledge of astronomy, I managed to pick out the star I wrote my unfortunate story on, only to have it torn down by scientific records— or rather, by this organization's manipulation of such records. To gain such influence would take countless years. Such devotion to a plan was almost unfathomable.

Then there was the length of time before the third star would become visible. Weiss and his men would all long be dead by the time their plan reached fulfillment. They must have truly believed in their plan, as surely as we believed in the need to stop them.

Lord John reached the top of the tower and scrambled to his feet. "That got the blood pumping, didn't it?" He hauled up the rope and detached it from the crenellation where it was tied. "We ought to hang onto this."

"Now we need to get inside," I said.

Traipsing into our enemies' base seemed like the height of foolishness and the opposite of the subtlety we'd employed thus far. I scanned the roof of the tower. A dark bundle sat at the base of the wall between two of the telescopes. I crouched alongside it to take a closer look.

Two black, hooded robes lay there, akin to the one Weiss wore. I picked them up. Although they weren't perfect, the sizes looked roughly appropriate for the two of us. Two white masks lay underneath.

So that was Professor Challenger's plan. With a grim smile, I tossed Lord John his robe and mask.

He cast a skeptical gaze at the items. "Are we really going to pass for a couple of educated cultists or whatever they are? Don't these chaps know each other?"

"The professor said Weiss makes them keep their identities secret from one another," I said as I pulled on my cloak. "That explains the masks. Still, I can't imagine they've avoided all forms of camaraderie, so we'd better avoid talking to anyone if we can help it."

He eyed his bow for a moment, then slung it over his shoulder before putting on his cloak.

Mine fit well enough, and when I lifted the hood, it concealed most of my face. I checked to make sure I could reach the package from Challenger even with the cloak on, and then I turned my attention to the mask. Its design was rather ghoulish, all white with only a tiny slit for the mouth and holes for the eyes. I fastened it and took a look at Lord John.

"I feel like a deuced idiot in this thing," he said from behind his mask.

Although the lack of humanity caused by not being able to see any facial features was a bit unsettling, our disguises should serve us well enough as long as we didn't say anything to give ourselves away. I scarcely recognized him myself. Even the slight bulkiness from his concealed bow and quiver were negligible due to the loose fit of the cloaks.

"Into the lion's den," he said. "You ready, young fellah?"

I nodded. "Let's find the professor."

The door into the tower swung open easily, and we took our first steps into the organization's base.

A narrow staircase wound downward into the tower's depths. The door closed behind us and left us in the dark, but tiny lights embedded into the walls illuminated the stairs. It created the illusion of being surrounded by a starlit sky, and the effect brought to mind a single word.

Obsession.

These people were obsessed with the unseen star, with the construct out beyond our planet. They'd devoted their lives to something they'd never seen and followed in the footsteps of people who had done the same all the way back to the days of those early texts that saw the Destroyer as a sleeping god. If anything, it grew worse over time, twisted from a fear of a destructive entity into the misguided ambition that this thing could be controlled.

The stairs reached a landing, and we stepped onto the tower's top floor. Ten doors led out of the central chamber. I opened one and peered inside. Five men, all dressed in cloaks and masks like ours, sat around a wooden table together. Papers covered the table, and there was no sound save for the scratching of their pens as they made furious notes and diagrams.

Five masked faces lifted, and I hastily closed the door.

"I don't know what's considered normal behavior around here," I said in a whisper to Lord John.

I could sense his smile behind his mask. "Checking every door almost certainly isn't. I say we head to the ground floor and see what we can find."

I didn't have a better plan for finding the professor, so I agreed.

Seven floors we descended in such a fashion, all of identical design, until at last we reached the floor with the larger outer door. The stairs continued downward, so presumably the tower had a basement as well.

Several cloaked men walked back and forth from one room to another, unlike on the silent upper floors. A few glanced at us, but no one stopped. Presumably they assumed we were among their number, and simply wondered what business we were on our way to perform.

The genius of these disguises struck me. With everyone's face concealed, they wouldn't realize we were extra unless everyone assembled together, which did not appear to be the norm. On the other hand, wandering around aimlessly might eventually attract attention.

Since we were on the ground floor, I checked one of the doors, but it again had a group of masked individuals huddled over books and documents, intent on what appeared to be calculations.

I glanced at the basement stairs and then at Lord John. He shrugged and nodded. It was the one floor we had yet to visit.

Even as I took a step toward the stairs, a door opened and the masked man who emerged walked straight toward us. Before I could do anything or provide an excuse to avoid a conversation, he grabbed us both by our shoulders and hauled us into the room he came from.

My heartrate returned to normal as he closed the door. His imposing build, the edge of black hair just barely visible under his hood—our assailant was none other than Professor Challenger.

"Was that quite necessary?" Lord John asked.

Challenger snorted. "You two fools were moseying about like schoolboys on a holiday. If I took the time to talk to you out there, you'd have probably given us all away."

"I thought we were fitting in quite well," I said.

"Did you, now? Then pray tell me how I was able to recognize you so quickly, since I hope at the very least you remember that your faces are hidden."

I winced. Challenger had snatched us away within a second of opening the door. His powers of deduction and intuition might have helped, but there must have been something to give him a sign.

"You two are about as well-suited to subterfuge as the average Londoner is to academic discussions," the professor grumbled under his breath as he strode across the room to sit at the table. "But you're dependable enough in other matters, so I'll try to have patience. Sit down and let us see if we can salvage this mission."

We sat across from him, and he opened up a journal.

By rights, he should have been as out of place as us—it was hard to imagine the loud, brash professor fitting in among this silent, introspective group. Yet if I'd seen him from a distance, I would assume he was no different than the others. He had adapted to this situation as easily as if he truly was one of them.

"I've been monitoring their efforts," he said, his voice low. "Fortunately, with the time drawing near, their work is difficult enough that they need to make use of the best minds they can turn to their purposes; even Weiss in all his paranoia no longer has the luxury of ignoring my genius when I offer it."

"Do you mean to say," Lord John asked, "that you've been *helping* these madmen?"

"A necessary sacrifice," Challenger said. "Since they've let me assist with their plans at higher levels, I've become privy to a great deal of information."

I understood the benefits, yet I shared Lord John's misgivings. The thought of Professor Challenger aiding such an effort was terrifying. "Couldn't you have… fed them false information instead?" I asked.

Challenger drew himself up and glared at us, the full force of his fury felt even through the mask. "It seems as though the two of you think I did not consider every possibility when I entered into this arrangement—that you assume you know better about what should be done, even though it was I who alerted you to this entire situation."

"I didn't—" I lifted my hands in protest, but the professor spoke over me.

"These men are highly intelligent, even approaching my own level. While they required my help in certain matters, any attempt at deceiving them would be detected over time, and right now that is what we can't afford."

"We can't afford to sit around arguing, either," Lord John said, "so let's get on with it."

"I most certainly agree," Challenger said.

I nodded. "Right, we're here to stop this thing, after all. I suppose it doesn't much matter if you helped them get this far when we won't let it go any further. What exactly are they planning?"

"From time to time, they hold 'ceremonies' in the basement, during which they use their equipment to send signals out into space. All of this follows the patterns recorded in the ancient texts that first alerted me to the nature of the Triad Awakening."

"Is there still time to stop them?" I asked.

He nodded. "The current 'ritual' has multiple parts, and this one is not yet complete. The next and final ceremony is planned for tomorrow night. As long as we stop them by tomorrow, they won't be able to finish their goal."

"That's all well and good," Lord John said, "but these chaps don't seem likely to give up. I suppose we could kill them all, but there are only three of us."

Challenger shook his head. "There are intervals of time in which the construct can receive these signals. If we prevent them from sending the signal tomorrow night, they won't be able to try again for thousands of years—and by then, the knowledge might be lost if we disrupt their activities well enough.

If not, we will at least have advance warning."

I nodded. At this point it had already occurred to me that in addition to writing up the truth about Danuk for the Daily Gazette, my account of these events would also serve to warn our descendants, although it could prove difficult to ensure they took it seriously.

"We will stay here until night falls," Challenger said. "Then we will sneak into the basement and destroy their equipment. We'll sabotage them so thoroughly; they'll never be able to salvage it in time."

"Then what?" I asked. "We escape?"

"You two will make your escape and get on the boat home before they can find you. I'll remain behind to feign ignorance and follow as soon as I'm able."

Lord John clapped his hands together. "Sounds like a plan. Get in, wreck their stuff, and get out again. Nice and simple."

"Have you been in the basement?" I asked.

"I have," Challenger said. "More importantly, I've also seen their plans and know the full details of the equipment they use. I know exactly what must be done."

For the first time since we'd arrived on Danuk, I truly relaxed. Being reunited with the professor restored my confidence. He'd planned everything out. Despite the odds against us, surely we couldn't fail.

"Now," he said, his tone dry, "considering the incompetence you two have shown at subtlety, it's probably for the best if—"

The door burst open.

My heart leaped into my throat as one of the masked men stepped inside.

"What is the meaning of this interruption?" Challenger asked.

"There's been a change of plans," he said. "We need to begin preparations for the ceremony immediately. It must be done today."

Professor Challenger rose from his seat. "What? The calculations showed it must occur tomorrow!"

"There was a mistake. We recalculated, and the time is now."

"A mistake?" Fury filled Challenger's voice, and for a moment it was like we were back home at a lecture hall while the professor debated academic rivals who thought they could take him down. "I handled those calculations myself, you doddering buffoon! Show me where I made a mistake, and I'll show you the mistake *you* made in your so-called recalculations!"

The other man held up his hands. "No, I'm not saying you made a mistake! Your calculations were perfect based on the information we gave you, but that's the problem."

"Explain," Challenger said.

"We mistranslated one of the ancient texts. Everything had to be adjusted, and since we've been off for this long, it's now imperative that we—"

Challenger stormed past him out of the room without waiting for him to finish.

The masked man faltered mid-sentence, then turned his attention to us. "I hope the two of you have no objections."

I shook my head, and to my vast relief, he left without expecting further conversation.

"Now things are getting interesting," Lord John said. An edge of excitement tinged his words. "So much for getting in and out without them noticing."

"Let's just hope the professor isn't causing too much of a scene," I said.

"It's rather nice to know the old boy treats them the same way he treats everyone else—what?"

We left the room together and followed the sounds of Challenger's bellowing until we found him in another room on the ground floor, where a group of masked men with notes and diagrams in front of them wilted under his rage.

"—all that work I went through," Professor Challenger shouted, "and now I learn you gave me incorrect information because you misread the texts you've studied for years. You call yourselves educated, learned men? Hah! How could people so devoted to your cause have blundered into a predicament like this? I thought here at least I'd distanced myself from such ineptitude, but you managed to amaze me with the truth that you're little better than any fool I could find wandering the streets of London!"

"Anyone can make a mistake," one of them said, with the weary tone of someone tired of being shouted at.

"A mistake? A *mistake*? Some mistakes are acceptable. There are times when one can afford to make mistakes. This is not one of those times! Something of this importance needs to be checked and double-checked. You got away with it this time because the ritual must be done tonight—what if you had gotten it so wrong that you learned it had to be yesterday… or judging by the sort of incompetence I can all so easily imagine, that it was months ago and we missed it entirely?!"

No one responded.

Challenger glared at them with such fury I almost pitied them.

"You are shortsighted, professor," said a cold voice from behind me.

I knew that voice.

Weiss stepped past us into the room. "Had we missed our opportunity, we would have simply left notes so that our successors would succeed in the future. It matters not whether we assembled here fulfill the Triad Awakening, as long as we pave the way for its success. We will never live to witness it, but we will never give up. Our order will live on for eternity."

A chill ran down my spine at the calm certainty in his voice. Yes, this was not the sort of man who could be reasoned with.

The others in the room nodded with murmurs of assent, and although Challenger continued to fume, he didn't argue.

"It is time," Weiss said.

Lord John and I fell in line behind Challenger as we followed the others out of the room and descended together into the basement.

More joined us along the way, and people packed the upper stairs. A few remained above, stationed as guards at the tower entrance, but it seemed almost everyone would be joining us down below.

As we neared the base of the stairs, the strange lights embedded in the walls gave way to metal and wires. The basement hummed with numerous machines, and several of the men with Weiss left to flip switches and ready equipment. Here, more than anything else on Danuk, all illusions about this place were stripped away to reveal its true nature.

More people pressed in on us from behind, and I was jostled by the sheer number of men joining us in the basement. Uneasiness crept through my confidence. We were outnumbered here, at the heart of their operation.

And since we would have to act, there was no way to avoid detection.

The men assembled in a circle around the machines, and I stepped awkwardly into a gap between two others. At least there was enough space, presumably for new recruits; perhaps they didn't have an accurate count of their number after all. I had gotten separated from my companions in the chaos, although when I looked around at the multitude, I could still pick them out. Challenger stood near the center of the circle with Weiss and a few who appeared to have positions of authority. He must have gained influence within their group, although not enough to convince them to abandon their foolhardy endeavor. As for Lord John, he stood on the opposite side of the circle as me, tense and poised with one hand partly under his cloak for the bow he'd taken from the village.

We stood there for a long time in silence. My impatience grew, but none of the others seemed perturbed. I watched the professor for any sign that he wanted us to act, yet he was silent. Everyone waited for the correct time to come, and the minutes stretched into what felt like hours.

"Begin," Weiss said at last.

At Professor Challenger's request, I will leave out the specific details of the machines located in the basement and how they worked. Too accurate a description might allow someone else in the future to replicate this organization's work and begin the Triad Awakening anew, whether out of arrogance or malevolence or the sheer curiosity that has been the undoing of

"Lord John and I fell in line behind Challenger..."

many good people.

Suffice it to say that their setup allowed them to send radio waves up through the tower, magnified many times to reach the far reaches of space and the distant construct.

The majority of the masked men began to chant, words which meant nothing to me but which had been passed down through millennia, their meaning misunderstood and reinterpreted over time, the syllables which together served as the activation code for the derelict machine high in the heavens. Others manipulated the equipment, modulating the signal in whatever way was necessary to accomplish their goal.

Challenger met my gaze and offered the slightest nod.

I looked around for the wires that connected the receivers to the broadcasting equipment. Once I spotted one, I looped my foot underneath it and wrenched it free.

One of the nearest men stopped his chant and rounded on me. "What do you think you're doing?"

I lifted my hands. "Accident."

"Be careful! We can't afford accidents today!"

I nodded and shuffled backwards as if in embarrassment, and slammed my elbow into another piece of equipment as I did so.

"Clumsy oaf!"

"I'm very sorry," I said.

On the other side of the room, Lord John purposefully strode from machine to machine with as much authority as those who activated them, and he undid what had been set up before him.

"That was the wrong way!" someone shouted at him.

"Was it now?" he asked. "It's so difficult to keep track."

I looked around for something else I might sabotage, but even as I took a step, the man who had confronted me grabbed my arm.

"Stand *still*," he said.

Meanwhile, three others moved between Lord John and the machines, and their voices rose as he argued with them that he was doing his job.

Weiss's voice cut over everything. "Enough!"

Everyone fell silent.

"What is this commotion? We can't have arguments corrupting the signal."

They all tried to explain at the same time, and Weiss looked from Lord John to myself with a silent intensity that made my skin crawl.

"I see," he said at last. "You must be the two men who escaped from the village."

My blood ran cold.

Lord John pulled out his bow and nocked an arrow. "Step away from the machinery, all of you! I daresay we've had enough your nonsense."

Unfortunately, his words had the opposite effect. The nearest men lunged for him. His shot got one in the leg even as two more tackled him. He rolled free, but he'd lost the advantage.

I dashed to the side as another tried to grab me, which brought me face to face with the man who'd confronted me over my sabotage. The time for subtlety had passed—I punched him in the jaw.

He went down, but we were vastly outnumbered.

"The ceremony!" Weiss shouted. "Subdue them, but keep the ceremony going! The signal must be sent!"

A smaller group clustered around him and resumed their chant, while others attempted to undo the damage Lord John and I had done. I ducked under a swinging punch and ran at the men reattaching the wires I'd disconnected, only to have someone grab me from behind. I jabbed my elbow into my assailant's stomach and broke free.

Professor Challenger's voice boomed throughout the cramped room. "Do you have any idea what you're doing?"

"That's right!" Weiss seemed unaware that the professor wasn't arguing in his favor. "You'll ruin everything we've worked toward!"

"No," Challenger said. "You are the fool for pursuing this endeavor. You attempt to grasp technology you have no hope of understanding, let alone controlling. I studied the ancient texts and the forgotten murals. You consider them priceless, but you ignore what they show—destruction!"

Weiss rounded upon him. "You! You're a traitor!"

"Only because you refuse to see reason."

It was surreal to hear their argument over the sound of our own raging conflict while Weiss's men formed a discordant harmony with their chant. A hooded man slammed me into the wall with jarring force to stop my progress. His hands closed around my throat, and my vision blurred. Suddenly, the pressure eased; I twisted free as he ripped an arrow from his shoulder. I met Lord John's gaze with a nod of gratitude and then darted back into the fray.

Lord John knocked over another piece of transmitting equipment, but soon he was surrounded by foes again.

"If you have any scrap of intelligence hidden away that hasn't been turned toward delusions of power," Challenger said, "think about what it would actually mean for the human race if that machine is activated."

Weiss only sneered in response. "Your fear is because of the records—records from ancient people so backward they saw this construct as a god. This is the modern era, *professor*, and by the time our signal reaches its destination, we will have advanced beyond your comprehension! Our successors will control it, and the world will enter a new age!"

"You will bring doom upon the entire human race in your arrogance!" Challenger roared.

I kicked my nearest attacker and shoved another away from me. The reconnected wires mere feet away taunted me with the danger they presented. Someone struck me from behind, their approach obscured by the hood and mask restricting my vision. As pain pulsed through my head, I tore off my mask and let my hood fall back. They already knew who we were, so there was no point in staying disguised.

A note of regret edged Weiss's voice. "I wanted to believe in you. You are a man of true vision."

"And you're an idiot." Challenger removed his own mask. "If you truly pay any heed to the words I say, then listen to me now."

"Oh no," Weiss said, "it is you who should be listening."

Around us, their chant reached a fevered pitch. With a bellow, Professor Challenger turned away from Weiss and charged at the men attacking me. His sudden action filled me with the urgent fear that we were almost out of time.

I dashed through the space he'd cleared and lunged for the wires. At last, my fingers closed around them.

I wrenched them free.

And silence descended over the room.

We all stood frozen. No one said anything; even the chant had ceased. Lord John breathed heavily, his mask lost during the chaos and an exhilarated half-smile on his face as he regarded our foes. I stood poised to move. These people had shown themselves to be ruthless. We needed to escape and find a way to survive until the boatman returned in the morning.

Then Weiss began to laugh. "Too late, my treacherous friends, too late. While you fought so bravely, the transmission went through."

My heart sank. We came this far… only to fail by mere fractions of a second.

Weiss stepped forward, to the transmitter that carried their voices into the heavens, and ripped a cluster of wires free himself. He dropped them and stamped his foot down upon them. "Don't think I trusted you completely, professor. I knew with the data you gathered in our service, a man of your capabilities might be able to deduce the ritual's meaning. At its core, it is a binary code; someone who studied both the ancient texts and the ceremony itself might be able to determine the correct sequence needed for *deactivation.* I also know about the equipment you had brought to your home. Yet just like us, you have a narrow window of time in which the command must be entered. You will not issue the deactivation code here, and you will never make it home in time—if you manage to leave this island at all."

That itself had begun to look unlikely. As Weiss's men closed in around us, Lord John retreated to our side. A sardonic smile twisted his lips. "Well, this has gone rather sour, hasn't it?"

"And now—" Weiss stopped.

Smoke crept down the stairwell and into the basement, merely a hint at first and then more. A muffled cry came from somewhere above us.

Footsteps pounded down the stairs, and one of the men who stayed as a guard burst in.

"What is happening?" Weiss asked.

"The village!" the man shouted between gasps for breath. "There's been a revolt—they're taking over the island. They're coming for us!"

Makalo! With Lord John and I making our move, he and the others dissatisfied with Weiss's control must have decided to take action as well.

Smoke poured in thicker than before. My eyes stung, and I covered my mouth with the edge of my cloak. Just like everyone had filled the basement room before, the mob pressed upward to reach the higher level.

At the ground floor, men raced toward the exit, but Challenger caught my arm before we could follow.

"Up the stairs!" he shouted. "To the top of the tower!"

I had no idea what he hoped to accomplish, but I didn't question it. Lord John and I sprinted for the stairs with the professor right behind us. While the others fled to escape the smoke, and sounds of combat reached our ears, we raced up each spiraling set of stairs.

Challenger had a plan, I was sure of it—and I needed to believe that plan would work. Even if Weiss were correct that humanity would advance enough to be able to control the mysterious machine once it activated, the thought of such power in the hands of his ilk boded little better than total annihilation if they failed to control it.

The narrow door at the top of the tower came into view, and I put on an extra burst of speed.

Fresh air came as a welcome relief after the stifling, smoke-filled air inside. I ran to the edge and the circle of telescopes. Down below, fires consumed the foliage around the base of the tower. A group of men fought at the doors, and despite the great distance, I recognized Makalo in the lead.

Yet he and his fighters were outnumbered. While Weiss's men were at a disadvantage due to the narrow entrance they emerged through, each one who made it tipped the balance in their favor. They were armed as well, and I could all too easily see this becoming a massacre.

"Let's even these odds," Lord John said. He lifted his borrowed bow and aimed at the men below. "Like hunting big game… although truth be told, I'd prefer the company of the lions."

His arrow hit its target, and one of Weiss's men fell.

"Quickly, Malone," Challenger said. "The package."

In all the chaos, I'd nearly forgotten the small box he entrusted to me before our journey. I retrieved it and tossed it to him. Our salvation, he'd called it, if the worst came to pass.

Challenger cast the packaging aside and opened the box. Inside rested a tiny radio transmitter.

Its construction was impressive, but I couldn't help but wonder what he hoped to achieve. No amount of genius could enable something so small to send a signal as far as Weiss's had gone.

Lord John let out a growl and nocked another arrow. Down below, a group of the masked men had cornered Makalo, and one was advancing toward him. "We'll see about that." He aimed and pulled the bowstring back.

A gunshot pierced the air, and Lord John dropped the bow as blood blossomed from his shoulder.

I whirled around.

Weiss stalked through the door toward us, his own mask askew to reveal cold gray eyes and a face framed by a fringe of blond hair, a gun in his hand. "You can't accept defeat, can you? These telescopes will show no sign of today's victory, but the Triad Awakening is complete, and nothing will stop us now."

"It's such a pity," Challenger said, "to see intelligence wasted on a man like you."

As they argued, Lord John retrieved his bow despite his injury. He looked grimly determined to aid the men below, and I realized the camaraderie he'd tried to forge with the young hunters was not wholly feigned.

Fury contorted Weiss's face as he regarded the professor. "I don't know what you think you can accomplish, but I see you're no better than those vermin down there, scrabbling against impossible odds in a futile attempt at survival." He raised his gun again. "Your time has come to an end, Professor Challenger."

In contrast, Challenger seemed almost completely calm. "Men like you will never win, because you cannot believe in anyone except yourself."

Weiss laughed. His gun was pointed straight at the professor's head. There was no hint of reluctance or hesitation in his demeanor. He would fire.

I charged toward Weiss, acting on instinct. The distance between us closed within seconds, even as his finger began to squeeze the trigger. He turned toward me, but I'd already reached him. I tackled him as though we were opponents in a rugby match. For a split second, his eyes widened with shock, and then the force of my momentum knocked him over the edge of the tower.

Weiss almost seemed suspended in the air, but then he hit the ground, limbs splayed outward, sightless gaze fixed upon the sky that held all his dreams, his ambitions ended forever.

For a moment, I stood frozen, staring down at what I had done.

Lord John let out a cry from where he peered over the other edge of the tower. "He's done it! Makalo has the upper hand!" He sagged back against the crenellations and let his bow drop. Blood soaked his shirt around his wounded shoulder, but he smiled in relief nevertheless.

I turned back to Professor Challenger. "What now?"

Challenger turned on the small radio and lifted it. "It's time."

On the other end, a voice said something I couldn't quite make out, and he nodded gravely in response.

"Yes," he said. "Please see that it is done exactly as I instructed you." Then he looked at us again. "Weiss was correct in thinking I'd replicated the tower's equipment and deduced the deactivation sequence in case it came to this, but his failure was his hubris. A man like Weiss would never expect me to rely on others, so he assumed we would need to send the signal ourselves."

My heart leapt. "Then, on the radio just now—"

He nodded. "I left instructions with my wife to explain the full story to Professor Summerlee once I departed for Danuk. Together with Austin, they have been waiting each day for my message. The three of them are issuing the deactivation code as we speak." Challenger lifted his head, as proud as I've ever seen him. "Gentleman, I'm pleased to say the threat of the unseen star is no more."

The three of us looked at one another, and after all the danger we'd overcome to reach this point, it was a relief to know this terrible incident was finally over.

With the death of their leader, the organization lost some of its fervor, and Makalo's faction was able to take full control of the island. Lord John led the efforts to round up Weiss's men and the loyalists from the village, and they were placed under armed guard.

A few days later, my own summarized account of events ran in the Daily Gazette.

DANUK'S DECEPTION REVEALED

"Readers may remember the controversy last year over the island of Danuk, which was said to be home to an isolated civilization that preferred to avoid contact with the outer world. In actuality, this was a lie perpetuated by an organization attempting to harness power through an elaborate plot discovered and thwarted by Professor George Challenger. The island itself had been under their control for quite some time, but thanks to the valiant efforts…"

And so on and so forth. I gave an abbreviated description of what we'd done on the island and, for my own vindication, mentioned the way the organization had altered those records about the new star in the sky.

What will happen to Danuk, I can't say for sure. Makalo has control of it for the time being, but I suspect he and his allies would prefer to return to their own homes once the situation on the island is straightened out.

I know it will be difficult for anyone to believe our story. People might take this to be a complete fabrication on our part, and indeed, we'll never be able to prove that an invisible threat in the sky posed such a danger to the human race. Yet if there's one thing I've learned over the years, it's that when Professor Challenger says something, it's wise to heed his warnings.

For my part, I'm content to know that our efforts were successful and the unseen star will never appear.

THE END

Creating
the Unseen Star

I first looked into Professor Challenger simply because I was curious about the sort of character who would have such a dramatic name. When I learned he was created by Sir Arthur Conan Doyle, I was even more intrigued. The creator of Sherlock Holmes had written a character described by some people as the "anti-Holmes"? I ended up buying a collection of the original Professor Challenger stories to see what they were all about.

The Lost World was an entertaining adventure that struck the core of what got me interested in pulp fiction in the first place, and I quickly moved on to the others (although admittedly I skimmed parts of *The Land of Mist,* which I found off-putting and almost mean-spirited toward its characters). The stories were exciting, the characters were likeable, and before I knew it, I was imagining the sort of story I might create with them.

Everyone wants to write about Sherlock Holmes, but I've always been a bit intimidated by the prospect. In contrast, Professor Challenger—somewhat ironically, since he's the more intimidating of the two—felt more approachable in his hotheaded, aggressive ways.

Now, I tend to have one foot firmly in Lovecraft's domain when I write short stories, and for quite a while I'd been puzzling over a vague story idea about a group of cultists trying to summon an ancient god that lies dormant in the far reaches of space. I didn't know what sorts of characters should face this threat, but the more I thought about it, the more I felt I'd found the right cast here with Professor Challenger. Those vague ideas slowly came together as the first draft of "The Unseen Star."

I expected Professor Challenger to be a difficult character to write, but while it certainly was a tricky balance to keep him likeable despite his aggressive nature and add the edge of humor usually present in his insults, the character who gave me the most trouble wasn't him at all, but rather Lord John Roxton.

Oh, Lord John. His peculiar speech patterns required an editing draft all of their own and created endless amusement for my first beta reader.

I hope I ultimately did Professor Challenger, Malone, and Lord John justice—but I'll let you be the judge of that.

In addition to those specific character details I paid attention to while revising "The Unseen Star," the story itself changed significantly between the original rough draft and the final version. Most notably, once I had decided upon this as a Professor Challenger story rather than straight-up cosmic horror, I needed to pull the ultimate threat more into the realm of science fiction… less "Cthulhu" and more *"Ancient Aliens,"* if you will.

This also led to a greater focus on the human antagonists. In the first draft, the organization's leader didn't even have a name; his group existed to enable the entity out in space, which in turn had a more immediate presence in the story. It was only in the second draft that "the tall cultist" developed into the paranoid, arrogant Weiss.

After all of these adjustments and revisions, I couldn't have finished "The Unseen Star" without the aid of my beta readers. They pointed out some of the more hand-waved science aspects, suggested ways to improve the story's pacing and development, and of course, helped me with the many problems posed by our dear Lord John.

I enjoyed stepping into the shoes of Malone for this adventure, and I hope his quest to help Professor Challenger stop the threat of the unseen star proved to be an entertaining one for all of you as well.

SAMANTHA LIENHARD—has been writing for most of her life, especially in the fantasy and horror genres. She graduated from Mansfield University with a B.A. in English and a minor in Creative Writing, and then from Seton Hill University with an M.F.A. in Writing Popular Fiction. When she isn't writing, she can usually be found playing video games. Her publications include a comedy novella called *The Zombie Mishap*, a Lovecraftian horror novella called *The Book at Dernier*, a Lovecraftian horror novelette called *It Came Back*, the pulp fiction story "The Domino Lady Takes the Case," and several short horror stories. She also writes for video games and has worked on the scripts for several indie titles, including *Ascendant Hearts, The Trials of Olympus III, Two Till Midnight,* and *Eternal Radiance.*

Information about all of Samantha's work can be found at her website: http://www.samanthalienhard.com